D0030214

To Henry—the next reader in our family

Beforever™

The adventurous characters you'll meet in
the BeForever books will spark your curiosity
about the past, inspire you to find your voice
in the present, and excite you about your future.
You'll make friends with these girls as you share
their fun and their challenges. Like you, they are
bright and brave, imaginative and energetic,
creative and kind. Just as you are, they are
discovering what really matters: Helping others.
Being a true friend. Protecting the earth.
Standing up for what's right. Read their stories,
explore their worlds, join their adventures.
Your friendship with them will BeForever.

TABLE *of* CONTENTS

chapter 1

Belle Isle

MELODY THOUGHT SHE'D never seen the sky as blue as it was today. The azure canopy arched over the Detroit skyscrapers rising silver in the distance. The May air was soft and scented with that special fragrance of damp earth and new leaves that only comes in the spring.

Melody bounced a little on the springy backseat of the Ford Fairlane as it sped past the shops and offices that lined the busy streets. She glanced over at her cousin Val sitting beside her. Val's mom, Tish, was driving them to a picnic.

Val grinned at Melody. "I'm so glad we're going to this picnic together, Dee-Dee," Val exclaimed. "I hardly see you anymore."

"Except for every week at church and every

Sunday for dinner," Melody teased, smiling. But what Val said was true. About one year ago, Val's parents had finally been able to purchase their own home in a nice neighborhood. It had taken them a long time, because many neighborhoods didn't want black families on their blocks. But the Fair Housing Committee, a group that was working to end this housing prejudice, had helped Tish and Charles, Val's father, find someone who was willing to sell to any buyer, regardless of race.

Melody was so happy for Val and her parents when they finally moved into their very own home. But Val's new house and school were farther away, and Melody missed her cousin. They couldn't walk home from school together the way they had when Val was staying with Melody's grandparents.

"Don't worry," Melody told Val. "It's not like I'm going to forget you. You're still my best cousin. We'll just have to make up for lost time when we *are* together."

"That's right, girls," Tish said over her shoulder. Her beehive hairdo shone in the sun pouring through the windshield. Tish owned a hair salon and always had the newest hairstyles. "You girls keep each other close. That's what families do."

The car wheels *thump-thumped* over the edge of the pavement and onto the steel girders of the MacArthur Bridge. Below them, the Detroit River glittered blue-brown in the sunlight.

"Woo-hoo! Belle Isle, here we come!" Melody called as they left the gritty city of Detroit behind. She craned her neck to spot the green leafy oasis of the park at the other end of the bridge. They were going to the spring picnic of the Fair Housing Committee at a park shelter on Belle Isle, a large island that sat right in the middle of the Detroit River. The entire island was a park.

"Belle Isle," Tish sighed as the park's huge trees came into sight. "This place is a rest for weary eyes."

Melody agreed. There was something special

about Belle Isle. Not twenty minutes from the car
horns and asphalt streets of Detroit, the grasses
and trees of the island fluttered in cool breezes. You
could do anything there—swim off the little sandy
beach, take a pony ride, watch the monkeys on their
gym at the children's zoo, walk through the woods—

"Mom, can we stop at the carousel?" Val's eager
voice interrupted Melody's reverie. "Dee-Dee,
remember how this was the first thing I wanted to
do when we moved here?" Val and her family had
lived in Birmingham, Alabama, until two years ago,
when they'd moved up north to Detroit.

"Yes!" Melody laughed. "You loved the silver
horse the best. Remember how we'd have to wait and
wait for that one to be free, and I'd be so impatient . . ."

"Forget about the carousel, baby, we can't stop
right now," Tish told them. "We'll be late for the
picnic, and we've got the meat. Everyone will be
wanting their hamburgers."

"We'll ride later," Melody told her cousin. "For

old times' sake. Look, there's the fountain!" The girls stared at the hulking gray stone fountain that spouted jets of water. They passed the band shell with its rows of benches, empty for now, and the ornate stone building that housed the aquarium.

"Oh, look at the conservatory in the sunlight!" Melody exclaimed. Tish slowed the car, and they all gazed at the vast glass-and-steel building that glittered like a massive diamond in the bright sunlight. The giant center dome was crowned with a cupola, with low greenhouses extending out either side—all built of glass so the exotic plants inside could grow in the heat and light. Lawns spread out around the main building and the greenhouses.

"Didn't you visit the conservatory with your school last year, Melody?" Tish asked as she started driving again.

"Yes," Melody said, "on a field trip." She remembered the musky, warm air inside the huge greenhouse. It had seemed like a blast of the tropics in the middle of a snowy Detroit winter. She recalled the towering palm fronds that brushed the ceiling, the giant pink hibiscus flowers thrusting their heads over the railings, and lavender wisteria that hung over archways like a gorgeous trailing curtain. Melody had never wanted to leave. Flowers and gardens were her favorite things—she loved digging in the soil, touching and smelling the flowers, helping living things to grow. Her grandfather, Poppa, loved flowers as much as Melody did—that's why he had his florist shop, Frank's Flowers.

"Here we are." Tish pulled up in a row of cars parked in front of a shady stone picnic shelter beside a grove of trees. A knot of adults stood around a smoking grill, the women in summer shifts, the men in short-sleeved shirts and straw fedoras. A few children chased one another on the grass, while some girls and boys sat on the picnic benches talking. "There's Phyllis," Tish said as she tugged a green metal cooler from the trunk. She nodded toward a tall woman wearing a yellow print dress. "She's the leader, you remember, Val?"

"Oh yes," Val said. "I remember she likes to talk . . . a lot," she murmured to Melody. Melody smothered a giggle. The housing group had helped Tish and Charles so much that Tish still attended the meetings. She often took Val, but Melody had never tagged along before.

More cars pulled up, spilling out their occupants—black and white, young and old—and soon the grill was full of sizzling burgers and hot dogs, their rich smoke wafting through the air and making Melody's mouth water. A few women spread a checked tablecloth on one of the picnic tables and set out big bowls of potato salad, Jell-O with pears, potato chips, and carrot and celery sticks. Coffee bubbled in a dented metal percolator at the side of the grill.

"I didn't realize the fair housing group had so many white people in it," Melody whispered to her cousin. "I thought it was just people from our church."

But Val didn't seem surprised. "This part of the housing group is called Operation Open Door," she said, taking a paper plate from the stack at one end of the table. "It's people from the churches and also the synagogues. So some of the people are Jewish."

Melody looked at the group with renewed interest. She'd never really talked to any Jewish people before, that she knew of. She did recall Big Momma, her grandmother, saying that their own neighborhood used to be mostly Jewish before it became mostly black.

"Let's eat, folks!" Tish called out a few minutes later, waving a metal spatula in her hand.

Everyone began lining up for food. Melody heaped her plate with Jell-O, chips, and a burger with lots of bright yellow mustard, and then followed Val over to one of the picnic tables, concentrating on her heaping plate. Suddenly, she collided with a tall white girl, almost tipping her meal into the grass.

"Whoops!" The tall girl grabbed Melody's plate with a lightning reflex. "Don't lose your burger!"

"Thanks," Melody breathed. The girl looked a couple of years older than Melody and Val, who were ten and twelve. She wore fashionable pink-flowered hip-huggers and a sleeveless pink blouse. Her flipped black hair was held back by a pink headband, and she even wore eyeliner. Melody thought she looked very sophisticated.

The girl smiled down at her, and Melody realized she was staring. "Thanks again!" she stammered and practically ran to the table where Val was already eating.

"Val, who's that?" Melody nodded at the tall girl, who was sitting a few tables away with a dark-haired woman who looked just like her. Melody figured the woman must be the girl's mother.

Val twisted around. "Oh, that's Leah. She's fourteen. Her mom's in the group, too—I think she knows my mother. They're from one of the synagogues, like I was telling you. I think they live in the next neighborhood over from you."

"She looks cool." Melody admired Leah's outfit again. She wasn't allowed to wear hip-huggers, but her big sister Yvonne, who was in college, had some. Then she turned back to Val and asked, "How come the Jewish people are on the housing committee?"

Val looked serious. "They've always worked on fair housing practices. Mom said that they had trouble buying homes once, too—people didn't want Jews in the neighborhoods the same way they don't want black people now. So we sometimes work together."

As Melody watched idly, the girl Leah leaned over and said something to her mother, who nodded. Leah slid off the picnic bench and walked rapidly away from the shelter in the general direction of the carousel until Melody couldn't see her anymore. Melody wondered where she was going—to the carousel? Well, maybe to the bathroom or something.

"Everyone! Your attention for a moment, please." The tall woman, Phyllis, stood up, and the talk died down. "Thank you all for coming to our spring picnic. We have such a delicious spread here. I just wanted to take a moment to update you on our efforts. As you know, we have been asking residents in key neighborhoods to sign Covenant Cards, which say that they will welcome people of any race or religion to their neighborhood. As of April, over three thousand Detroiters and one thousand suburban homeowners have signed. This is a great success!"

Everyone clapped and cheered, and Melody felt her heart lift. She remembered feeling the same way last year when she and her family marched in the Walk to Freedom and heard Martin Luther King speak. It felt like everyone was joined together for the same goal: fairness and equality.

Phyllis spoke over the applause. "We must not let our efforts cease! I have fliers here letting residents know that our volunteers will be coming to their neighborhood asking for Covenant Card signatures. We will need to distribute these fliers this week."

"Ooh, I can do that," Val murmured to Melody. "I could go after school."

"I'll help you," Melody assured her.

Phyllis sat down, and everyone started talking and eating again. The wind rustled the leaves, and a cool breeze off the river blew across the back of Melody's neck. Val was chattering about handing out the fliers, but Melody was watching the girl with the stylish pink bell-bottoms, Leah, coming back up the paved path. She walked with her shoulders straight and her tanned arms swinging. Melody thought she looked like the model on the cover of the *Teen* magazine she'd seen last week at the drugstore. Leah slid onto the bench beside her mother and pulled her plate toward her.

Suddenly, as if she felt Melody's eyes on her, Leah turned and smiled at her. Melody looked away, embarrassed at being caught staring again, but Leah rose from her place and came over to Melody's table, carrying her plate of half-eaten food.

"Hi," she said, sitting down on the bench beside Val, across from Melody. "Do you mind if I join you? I think our mothers are perfectly happy without me." She gave a tinkling laugh and nodded toward Tish and the dark-haired woman, now vigorously discussing something. "I'm Leah," she told Melody.

Melody smiled. "I'm Melody. Thanks again for rescuing my lunch."

"How's your new house?" Leah asked Val. Delicately, she forked up a bite of potato salad. "Do you like it?"

"Yeah, it's great," Val said. "I love having my own room. We painted it pink."

Leah sighed. "Oh, that sounds so pretty. Pink's my favorite color. Mom painted mine gray. Except she called it 'pearl.' Call it what you want, it's still gray."

"You could pretend you're living in a cloud," Melody suggested. Leah laughed, and Melody felt a flush of pride. Leah thought she was funny, or maybe clever. "I like your hip-huggers," she told Leah. "I wish I was allowed to wear those."

"Thanks," Leah said. "Believe me, I had to beg long and hard to get Mom to make me some. She wanted me to buy my own pair with some of my babysitting money."

"Babysitting would be fun," Melody exclaimed. "I'd like to babysit to have a little extra spending money. And babies are so cute."

"Yeah." Leah hesitated. "But I'm saving up for something more important than clothes. Anyway—" She jumped up. "Let's go ride the carousel. You want to? I'll just go tell my mom."

"Great!" Melody jumped up too.

To her surprise, Val frowned a little. "I thought we were going to ride the carousel just you and me," she murmured to Melody as Leah strode over to her mother.

"Well, why not Leah, too?" Melody asked. "She's so nice. Come on, let's go ask your mother." Melody hurried over to join Leah without waiting for Val's answer.

The carousel was spinning merrily when they arrived, filled with shrieking children all clutching the brass poles and riding up and down on the brightly painted horses. The calliope music slowed and stopped just as they walked up. The scowling man who ran the ride clanked the metal gate open as the children filed off.

"We used to ride this when Val first moved here," Melody told Leah as they lined up and handed over their dimes. "Back then she always wanted the silver horse."

Val nudged Melody and gave her a look.

What? Melody mouthed. Val frowned and looked away.

"Aw! That's so cute," Leah was saying, smiling at Val. "Hey, there's your old friend." The girls followed Leah as she quickly wove through the animals until she came to the silver horse. "Hop on!" she patted his worn black saddle.

"That's okay," Val said a little stiffly. "That was when I was little. I don't care what color I get now, obviously." She climbed onto a yellow horse, while Melody chose a prancing red one.

"I used to come here with my grandfather," Leah shouted over the music as the carousel started and their horses rose and fell. "He always liked the lion."

"Was that when you were a little kid?" Melody called, clinging to her pole. The horse was more slippery than she remembered.

"Yeah. He could get around better then." Leah's voice dropped so that Melody had to strain to hear it over the music.

"Is he crippled?" she asked.

But Leah only looked straight ahead, her lips folded tightly together in a line so straight it looked like a slash across her face. Melody was pretty sure Leah had heard her. Why didn't she answer?

Suddenly Melody felt awkward. Maybe Leah's grandfather *was* crippled—and maybe it had been insensitive of her to ask Leah about it.

When the ride stopped, the girls made their way back from the carousel on the paved path that wound through the zoo. The noisy gibbons sounded like a flock of birds, and llamas gazed at them through long-lashed eyes. They paused to watch the baby elephant get a bath from a hose, then wandered slowly on toward the aquarium and the conservatory. The air was hot now and humming with the sleepy drone of midday insects. As they passed a playground, swing chains clanged and little children shouted and scrambled over a metal jungle gym. The doors of the aquarium were propped open, and people streamed in and out.

Leah and Melody chatted as they walked. Leah was easy to talk to, Melody thought, and she laughed a lot. Melody noticed, though, that Val was unusually quiet.

Leah veered off the sidewalk. "Here, let's cut through by the conservatory. This way leads right to the shelters." The noises of the zoo and the playground faded as the girls padded through the short, thick grass. Gardens rose around them, lush and fragrant in the humid air. Leah led the way confidently, like a forest guide, weaving between flower plots with rows of tulips and clumps of huge ornamental grasses. Through the tree branches, Melody could just see the silvery walls of the conservatory rising into the sky.

"Oh, this is so pretty," she breathed. "I've never been back here."

"Are we even supposed to be going this way?" Val asked from just ahead of her. "There's no path or anything."

"It's okay!" Leah called from ahead. "It's just a shortcut."

The girls walked single file, pushing through the tall dry grasses left from last year. A yellow and black butterfly lit on a shrub covered with purple flowers, and Melody slowed to inspect its intricately patterned wings opening and closing. She bent down so that her eyes were level with the insect. Its two black antennae waved delicately. Melody caught her breath as the butterfly's black tongue, slender as a hair, unrolled to taste the center of one of the purple flowers.

"Val," Melody murmured. "Look at this."

But her cousin did not answer. Melody raised her head. She was alone. Val must have thought Melody was still behind her or she wouldn't have gone ahead.

Melody looked around. The corridor of flowers was deserted. "Val!" she called. "Leah!" But there was no answer.

Melody hurried through the shrubs and flowers, but whatever map Leah was following in her head was invisible to her. Melody followed a faint trail that she thought would lead to the shelters and the river, but she found herself wandering in an apple orchard, frosted thickly with fragrant white blossoms. Then abruptly, the trees cleared, and the conservatory loomed in front of her.

"Definitely not the right way," Melody murmured to herself. But she knew that if she went around to the front entrance, she could follow the sidewalk back to the park shelters. She trotted across the expanse of lawn and toward the side of the huge glass building. Leah and Val were still nowhere in sight, but a man stood bent over by a side door in front of her. The door was shut, and he appeared to be inspecting the doorknob. The air was very still.

"I think the entrance is around the front," Melody called out.

The man straightened up. He was nicely dressed in a brown suit. His red hair was brushed back under a tan fedora. His face was smooth and bland. "Thank you, little girl," he said quietly. "I seem to have taken a wrong turn." He walked off around the side of the building.

Melody squinted at the door the man had been looking at. The shiny metal handle was smudged with fingerprints as if he had been trying to open the door.

Melody walked around to the front of the building, the same way the man had gone. When she reached the front sidewalk, Val and Leah were waiting for her, waving. But the man was nowhere to be seen. Maybe he hadn't really been looking for the front entrance.

"Hurry up, Melody!" Val looked annoyed, but also slightly worried.

"We thought you got lost," said Leah.

"Sorry," said Melody. "Come on, let's get back

to the picnic." She sighed as they hurried along the walk. "I love the conservatory."

"Me too!" Leah agreed. "Have you seen the giant ferns?"

"Yes!" Melody remembered the giant, towering fronds.

"The birds-of-paradise are my favorite." Leah's face was lit up. "Blue—"

"And orange!" Melody broke in. "I love them, too! My grandpa had one in his flower shop once— remember, Val?"

"Um . . ." Val looked blank. "Was that the little tree thing he had?"

"No, that was a rosebush in a pot!" Melody laughed. She turned back to Leah. "And did you know there are orchids there? There's a whole orchid room. I haven't seen it, but I bet it's beautiful."

"Yeah!" Leah agreed. "They're gorgeous, and so many different kinds—moth orchids and boat orchids and cattleyas and vandas—"

"Wow!" Melody was impressed. "You really know about orchids! I know more about plants that grow around here. I have a book that has orchids in it, but I've never seen one in real life before." Melody's well-worn copy of *Plants of the World* had been on her bedside table since Poppa had given it to her three years ago, and she liked looking at the orchid pictures. Some of the blossoms looked like exotic spotted butterflies, others like fancy purses.

"Orchids are so neat," Leah said, enthusiasm bubbling in her voice. "There's a chocolate orchid that smells just like chocolate, and there's one called the white egret orchid. It's my favorite. It looks like a bird spreading its wings. And the monkey orchid actually looks like there is a tiny monkey face in the middle of the flower."

"And some of them are very rare, right? That's what my book says."

Leah paused. "Yeah. And the rare ones can be worth a lot of money. Not many people know that."

She shot Melody a strange glance and walked a little faster. Her cheeks were red.

Melody started to ask Leah what was wrong, but she had a sudden feeling Leah didn't want her to. Anyway, they were almost back to the picnic shelter.

chapter 2
Flowers and Family

"DINNER, MY CHICKS!" Melody's grandmother, Big Momma, called as she carried a big dish
of pot roast from the kitchen. "Melody, will you put
the napkins out?" Big Momma wasn't very big at
all, but the whole family called her that as a way of
showing respect for the oldest mother in the family.

Melody distributed paper napkins at each place,
while her older sister Lila filled the water glasses.
Melody's family always had Sunday dinner together
at Big Momma's after church, and it was Melody's
favorite time of the whole week. She loved the sight
of her family's faces gathered around the table.

"Here, Mama, let me do that," said Melody's
mother. Tying a yellow-checked apron over her
navy blue church dress, she took the heavy dish

from Big Momma, set it down on a trivet, and began spooning potatoes, onions, and carrots into a big bowl beside it. "Melody, call your daddy, will you?"

Melody opened the screen door off the kitchen and stepped outside. Daddy was out there with his head under the hood of the Ford, tinkering. "Daddy, dinner," Melody called.

Her father wiped his hands on a rag and draped his arm around Melody's shoulders as he came up the steps. "Let's get some of that pot roast. I've been smelling it for the last half hour."

"Where's Poppa?" Melody asked.

"Right here!" Melody's grandfather's voice rang from the doorway as he came in carrying a big cardboard box.

"Come get your dinner, Frank," Big Momma fussed. "Your meat is getting cold."

"I just picked these beauties up from my supplier. Didn't have time to drop them at the shop yet." Poppa set the box down on the coffee table.

Melody could see it was full of small potted plants full of ruffly, deep pink flowers.

Mommy, Daddy, Lila, Big Momma, Poppa, and Melody gathered around the table. The gathering was smaller than usual. Her oldest sister, Yvonne, was away at college, and her big brother, Dwayne, was touring with his Motown group, The Three Ravens. Val's family was also missing the Sunday dinner. Aunt Tish was repainting her salon and needed Val and Charles to help so she could be open the next day.

"Say grace, will you, baby?" Big Momma asked Melody.

Melody closed her eyes. "By Thy hands must we be fed. Give us, Lord, our daily bread." She let the familiar words linger on the air.

"Are those begonias, Poppa?" Melody asked her grandfather as the gravy boat, bowls of corn and peas, and basket of rolls began making their way around the table.

"They are!" Poppa poured fragrant gravy over his meat.

"I've never seen ones like those before," Melody said. She dished some corn onto her plate. "They look fancy."

"They're for the Belle Isle Conservatory Flower Show. It's next weekend." Poppa took a bite of meat and patted his gray mustache with his napkin. "Our flower club is sponsoring the show this year, and I'm going to have a booth there to display some of the best bouquets and potted flowers from the shop."

"Hey, I was just at the conservatory yesterday!" Melody exclaimed. "Well, outside it. For the Fair Housing Committee spring picnic with Tish and Val."

"Yes, how was the picnic?" Mommy asked, refilling Daddy's coffee. "Did you learn something?"

"Well, I met some people from the synagogues there." Melody looked around the table.

"What, you mean Jewish people?" Lila asked. "On the Fair Housing Committee?"

Mommy nodded. "Jewish people and black people have worked together on issues like this for a long time," she said, sounding like the teacher she was.

"Did you know that one of the founders of the NAACP was Jewish?" Daddy asked. He sipped his coffee.

"That's the National Association for the Advancement of Colored People," Lila told Melody.

"I *know* that," Melody told Lila. But she hadn't known that one of the founders was white, or Jewish.

"From the start, Jewish people have worked on civil rights. Rabbis marched arm in arm with Dr. King in Selma, Alabama, during the freedom marches this spring," Mommy added.

"I also met a new girl at the picnic. Her name's Leah. She's white—she's from one of the synagogues, and I really like her," Melody told the family. "Can she come over sometime, Mommy?"

"Of course she can, honey," Mommy said. "Any of your friends are welcome at our house."

"Well, don't get too busy," Poppa said, holding up his hand. "I'm going to need some help next weekend."

"I'll help you, Poppa!" Melody exclaimed. She loved helping Poppa in his shop. "What do you need me to do?"

"What I need is an assistant at the flower show," Poppa said. "I need someone with experience, some-one I can rely on, someone . . ." He pretended to look around the table as if considering his options. "Ah! Like you!" Poppa pointed at Melody, and she giggled at his joke. "I can't think of a better assis-tant. Come out to Belle Isle in the truck with me on Friday, and we'll set up the booth together. And—" Poppa smiled at Melody with his eyes crinkling. "I hear there's going to be a fancy party on Saturday at the conservatory for the flower club members—and their dates. It's called the Saturday Night Soiree."

"Oh!" Melody dropped her roll on her plate. "Poppa, Mommy, do you think I can go?" She looked hopefully from grandparent to parent.

Poppa smiled mischievously. "Well, I guess we'll just have to wait and see if you get an invitation to the Soiree, now, won't we?"

chapter 3

Friends and Fliers

TUESDAY AFTER SCHOOL, Melody trotted down her porch steps as Val hopped out of her family's Ford Fairlane and slammed the heavy door with a *clunk.*

"Bye, Daddy!" Val called.

Charles leaned across the seat and spoke through his open window. "Now, you girls be careful. The neighborhood you're going to is mostly friendly to black people, but not every person is. I'll pick you up back here in an hour or so, baby."

Val waved at her father, and the station wagon pulled away from the curb.

"Hey, cousin," Val said. "Have some fliers!" She pulled a stack of fair housing fliers from the bag slung over her shoulder, and the girls headed down the sidewalk.

The day was crystal blue with puffy white clouds sailing overhead. On the tidy lawns, tulips nodded their red and yellow heads, while the last of the crabapple petals sprinkled the sidewalk at their feet. They passed the chain-link fence of the park they'd fixed up last summer with their friends. Melody got a little burst of pride every time she saw the bright metal jungle gym and new swings. The morning glories she'd planted around the base of the swings were starting to twine up the metal poles, getting ready for summer, when their blue horn-shaped flowers would burst forth.

About half a dozen blocks away, the girls turned right. They were out of Melody's neighborhood now. The houses were larger here, big wooden and brick homes that had once been fancy, with large porches and bay windows. Some had been converted to apartments and had two or three mailboxes on the front porch. At one house, a white woman was collecting her mail. She glanced over her shoulder at the girls and frowned, then disappeared through her front door.

"Is this where we're stuffing the mailboxes?" Melody asked, suddenly feeling a bit nervous.

"Yep," said Val confidently. "This is the neighborhood."

"Hey, did you say Leah lives here? Maybe we'll see her." The thought of a familiar face was comforting.

Val shrugged and didn't say anything else.

Melody looked at her cousin for a long moment. She could tell that something about Leah was bothering Val. But whatever it was, Val wasn't saying—not yet, anyway. Melody examined the fliers Val had handed her.

"Fair Housing for All!" the headline at the top trumpeted. "Help Integrate Our Neighborhoods." Then, in smaller type, "The Greater Detroit

Committee for Fair Housing Practices works to help families of all races become homeowners. Would you be willing to sell your home to a Negro family? If so, look for a Covenant Card in your mailbox soon! Sign the card and become part of our movement!"

"This is it." Val counted the fliers rapidly. "Fifty. Let's see if we can deliver them all before Daddy picks me up." Her face was lit with an intensity Melody couldn't remember seeing before.

"This is really important to you, isn't it?" Melody said to her cousin as they climbed the first set of steps and poked a flier through a mail slot. "You were so sad last year, when you all couldn't find a house to buy."

Val nodded. "I wanted to us to have a place of our own, like your family does."

Melody squeezed her cousin's arm as they walked. "Well, now you're in your very own house."

"That's right—so now it's *my* turn to help some

other people who're having the same problems." Val smiled and lifted her chin.

"Well, I'm glad I'm helping, too." Melody looped her arm through Val's and pulled her cousin close against her side as they crossed a lawn to a house with peeling lavender paint and sagging lace curtains at the windows. Inside, a dog barked repetitively, as if he'd been wound up.

"Oh hey, speaking of mail . . ." Melody pulled a small cream-colored card from her pocket. "Mommy said Poppa sent you one of these, too!"

Val read the card aloud. "'Join Us for Our Saturday Night Soiree! 15th of May, 1965. 7:00 p.m., Belle Isle Conservatory. Sponsored by the Detroit Metro Flower Fanciers. Semiformal Attire.' Yes! I got one, too, this morning. We're going to be Poppa's dates!"

"I think I'm going to wear my pink dress, the one with flowers on it. You remember that one?" Melody slipped a flier into the crack of a storm door.

A white woman opened the door suddenly, startling Melody so that she jumped. The woman was older, with a doughy face and cat-eye glasses. "What's this?" she snapped suspiciously, unfolding the flier with a shake. Melody's stomach sank. Val's father had warned them that not everyone would be friendly.

The woman scanned the flier. "And where are these cards?" she demanded, tapping the paper as if it had done her some injustice.

"Uh, we don't have them right now, ma'am," Val stammered. Her eyes were big. Melody could hear her voice shaking a little. "We—we're supposed to bring them next week."

"It would be more efficient if you brought them now, missy," the woman said. "Now, I expect one delivered to my house. And you girls stand up straight when you speak to people. Look them in the eye. Half of these old cranks won't give you the time of day unless you put yourself out there." She fixed the girls with a glare. Melody inhaled and straightened her shoulders. "Better," the woman said brusquely. "Now, get back to your work." She banged the front door in their faces.

The girls skittered off the porch so fast that Melody almost fell down the steps. Once they were safely on the sidewalk, she and Val looked at each other and burst into giggles, holding on to each other for support.

"Oh my, I thought she was mad that we were there!" Melody gasped.

"But instead, she was just mad that we weren't doing a good enough job." Val wiped her eyes. "I guess I didn't expect that, because she's a white lady."

"Yeah," Melody agreed. "You can never tell what's on the inside of people." She thought fleetingly of Leah.

"We only have twenty fliers left," Val said. "Come on, we better tackle the rest of these houses." She hurried down the sidewalk.

Melody followed. As they passed an alley, she heard raised voices and turned to look. Two people were arguing heatedly—a teenage girl and a man in a hat. She could only see the man's back, but the girl—Melody stopped. The girl looked just like Leah—it *was* Leah, Melody was sure of it! Leah's voice was high, and she was gesturing rapidly, while the man replied in a smooth, deep baritone.

"Leah, hi!" Melody called out. She waved, smiling. Leah looked over, but her face was not happy. She said something to the man, and he stepped aside.

Leah hurried over to Melody and Val, her face flushed. "Hey, I'm busy, okay?" she said shortly. "I'll catch up with you later." She looked flustered.

"Oh, okay." Melody backed away, stung by Leah's sudden prickliness. "Yeah, of course." She cleared her throat, trying not to look hurt.

Leah turned around and scurried back to the man waiting in the shadows. Melody and Val set off down the sidewalk again.

"Guess she didn't want to see us," Val remarked.

"She said she was busy," Melody murmured. She kept her face neutral. She didn't want to give Val a reason to dislike Leah. But she couldn't help wondering what Leah was doing, talking to some man in an alley. Was she in some kind of trouble?

Melody accompanied Val up and down a few more porches, her mind still puzzling over Leah and the man, only half-listening to Val's stream of chatter about school.

"Hey, Melody! Hi, Val!" It was Leah, now running toward them. She caught up to them with a big smile on her face. "What are you girls doing?"

"We're passing out these fliers for Covenant Cards." Melody showed her one, eyeing Leah closely. Leah looked as sleek and sophisticated as ever in a short plaid jumper and mustard-yellow turtleneck, her long hair held back with tortoiseshell barrettes. Why was she being so friendly now, when she'd just told Melody to back off five minutes before?

"Oh yes, these are really important," Leah agreed. She took a handful of fliers. "Here, I'll help you."

The sidewalk wasn't quite wide enough for three. Melody didn't know how it happened, but somehow, she and Leah wound up walking together, while Val followed behind them. It felt uncomfortable, almost as if she and Leah were leaving Val out, although it wasn't on purpose.

"—grandfather wanted to rent, but they told him, 'No Jews allowed!'"

"What?" Melody tuned back in to what Leah was saying.

"I was just saying that when my grandfather first came to Detroit, he needed to rent an apartment," Leah said. "But no one would rent to him. Every place he tried, they'd tell him Jews weren't allowed in that neighborhood."

"That's just like what happened to Val's family last year!" Melody said. "Right, Val?"

"Yeah. That's right," Val said quietly.

"My grandfather had just immigrated to America from Krakow, Poland, where he was a botany professor," Leah continued. "That's a professor of plants. Orchids were his specialty." Leah's voice trembled suddenly. She folded her lips in a strange tight line. *Just the way she did on the carousel when she talked about her grandfather,* Melody thought. But in another instant, the moment had passed as swiftly as it had come.

"That's how my mother and I got started on the Fair Housing Committee," Leah went on. "When we heard Beth Elohim—that's our synagogue—was organizing a group, we knew we had to join. And I'm so glad we did, because I got to meet you two!" Leah squeezed Melody's arm. Her touch was like a warm glow. Melody beamed and looked over at Val hopefully. Leah and Val really did have things in common. Did Val see that? But her cousin didn't say anything at all.

Leah looked from Val to Melody and back

again. She took her hand off Melody's arm. "Um, Val," she said softly, "you're awfully quiet. Do you not want me around?"

"No!" Melody said right away. "No, of course we do!" She nudged Val with her foot. Her cousin was being rude, and now she was hurting Leah's feelings. "Come on, please help us with the rest of the fliers."

They finished delivering the fliers at the end of the block, and Leah stopped in front of a yellow house with a wide white porch. "This is where I babysit." Three little children's faces appeared at the front windows. "I sit for the Myers three days a week until five." A little girl squished her face side-ways against the glass and stuck out her tongue.

"Lucky you," Melody giggled.

Leah sighed, but she was smiling. "It's not so bad. I have a secret weapon." She pulled three Baby Ruth candy bars from her purse. "Well, gotta go. Hey, you two should come home with me sometime.

You could meet my grandfather. And you could see his orchid, too—it's really rare. He brought it with him from Krakow. It's a slipper orchid."

"Ooh, I would love that," Melody breathed. She felt honored by the invitation. "I'll ask my mother." Val was silent.

"Great!" Leah waved. "Tomorrow I don't babysit, so I'll meet you on 12th Street after school." She opened the Myers' door, and a chorus of little voices swelled with excitement.

Quiet settled after Leah disappeared into the house. Melody and Val stood on the sidewalk, not moving. Melody glanced at her cousin, who seemed to be studying the bark pattern on the nearest tree. Melody cleared her throat. Her stomach felt fluttery. She hated it when she and Val had a difference of opinion.

The girls began walking back toward Melody's neighborhood in silence. Melody's shoes sounded abnormally loud to her ears.

"We were going to make brownies at Big Momma's tomorrow," Val said finally. "I guess you'll be busy, though."

Melody bit her lip. She'd forgotten about the brownie date. "I can still make brownies," she assured Val. "I won't stay long at Leah's. Just an hour or so. We'll have lots of time to bake."

"Well, I guess I don't see why you're making friends with her," Val burst out. "We've got plenty of friends already."

"And I don't see why you have to be so jealous," Melody snapped. She saw Val wince at the word and immediately wished she could take it back.

"I'm not!" Val protested weakly.

"Yeah, you are," Melody said. "You won't hardly talk to her, and you make a face every time *I* say anything to her."

"I don't get why you like her so much." Val jabbed at the crosswalk signal at 12th Street, busy with late-afternoon traffic.

"I just do," Melody said. "I think she's neat. She's cool and smart and she knows about things."

"Maybe," said Val. "But she's—she's white."

"I can see that," Melody retorted. "Why should it make any difference that she's white? You're friends with Cindy." Cindy was the girl who lived next door to Val, and Cindy was white.

Val shook her head. "That's different. Of course I'm friends with her—she lives right next door. But this Leah is just butting in, getting between you and me, inviting you to her house."

"She invited you, too!" Melody pointed out.

"We both know that invitation was meant only for you."

"Well, maybe you should try being nicer to her." Melody fought down her annoyance. "I mean, if you don't want to be friends with Leah because she's white, isn't that like some girl saying she doesn't want to be friends with us because we're black?"

"It's not the same!" Val snapped. Melody took a step back. Her cousin's eyes were wide and her cheeks were red. "Look, you don't know what we saw in Birmingham. People were beaten up—even *killed*—for being friends with white people."

"Hey, hey, okay," Melody said soothingly. "I'm sorry." She hugged her cousin. "I get what you're saying. But you don't have to be afraid up here. And Leah is really nice. And she cares about fairness and stopping prejudice, same as we do. Okay?"

Val swiped a hand across her eyes. "Sure, but I still don't see why that means you have to be all buddy-buddy with her," she mumbled.

Melody followed her cousin across the street. In front of the library, she grabbed Val's hand. "We're cousins, Val. That makes us special—like friends but even better. Just because I have other friends doesn't change that." She squeezed Val's hand encouragingly and reached out to brush away a crabapple petal that had fallen on her shoulder.

Val didn't say anything, but Melody heard her sigh. Val started walking again.

Melody stood, watching her cousin's back. Her stomach felt hollow with worry.

Then Val turned. "Well, come on," she called. "What are you just standing there for? You know Big Momma's making oatmeal-raisin cookies for us when we finish giving out fliers. If you don't hurry up, I'm going to eat them all myself."

Melody exhaled and smiled. She hurried after Val. The argument was finished for now. But Melody worried that it wasn't over for good.

chapter 4

The Lady's Slipper Orchid

"WELL, HELLO!" LEAH'S mother opened the door of the apartment and greeted Melody, who was still trying to catch her breath after climbing three flights up a dark stairwell. Leah had met Melody at 12th Street after school, as promised, and the girls had walked back to Leah's apartment together. Now Leah ushered Melody into a small living room.

"Mom, you remember Melody from the Fair Housing picnic," Leah said, introducing them. "You know Tish Porter and her daughter, Val? Melody is their cousin."

"Oh, yes, of course I do!" Mrs. Roth said. "Tish and I have worked together for several months now. It was nice to meet her daughter Val at the picnic

49

last week—and it's nice to meet you, too, Melody."

"Thank you," Melody said politely, trying not to stare at the apartment. She'd never seen a room like this one. The walls were covered in big framed posters of modern art. The coffee table and side tables held little enameled bowls and vases. A large candlestick with seven arms, branched out like a tree, sat on the sideboard, with two silver candlesticks and a silver wine cup beside it. A six-pointed star was carved on the wine cup. The star looked as if it was made of two triangles, one upside down on top of the other. The synagogue Melody had seen in the neighborhood near hers had a big star just like it carved on the front of the building.

"You want a snack?" Leah led Melody into a small kitchen with a yellow linoleum floor. Melody smiled when Leah started slapping peanut butter on bread. It seemed as if everything would be different here, but Leah was making peanut butter

on Wonder Bread, the same after-school snack as
Melody had at home.

"I'm making you girls a little treat," Mrs. Roth
said from the stove, where she was stirring something in a strange-looking pot. It was taller than
it was wide, and it had a short, fat handle sticking
out one side and a lip for pouring. "Do you like hot
chocolate, Melody?"

"Yes, thank you," Melody said in her best
company voice. When she and Leah took their
sandwiches to the table, she remembered to sit up
straight and put her napkin in her lap, just the way
Mommy taught her.

Leah's mother poured a thick stream of creamy
chocolate into their mugs. "I hope you like this
chocolate, Melody," she said. "It's Mexican, so it
has a little cinnamon in it—and even a little hot
pepper."

Pepper in the hot chocolate? Melody looked
across at Leah, who nodded her head. "Try it. Mom

found it at the Mexican market. It's really good."

Melody sipped and then smiled. "It's delicious," she told Mrs. Roth. She patted her lips neatly with her napkin.

Melody and Leah sipped and munched while Mrs. Roth washed carrots and scrubbed potatoes at the sink. It looked like she was making beef stew, same as Big Momma. Over Leah's shoulder, pinned to the refrigerator with a magnet, Melody noticed a piece of paper with some kind of strange writing on it. It looked like a worksheet, but Melody couldn't read a word on it.

"Leah, what's that?" Melody asked, pointing to the sheet of paper.

Leah twisted around. "Oh, that's my Hebrew school homework." She made a face. "I have to read that passage in Hebrew and answer questions about it."

"Wow, you can read Hebrew?" In her Sunday school class, Melody had learned that the Bible was originally written in Hebrew, but it seemed amazing that Leah could actually read those odd blocky shapes.

Leah tipped up her mug to catch the last drops of hot chocolate. "Come on, I'll show you my room." The girls rinsed their cups in the sink, and Melody followed Leah down a narrow, dark hallway to the back of the apartment.

Leah's room was small and neat. A single bed was covered with a cheery yellow-flowered bedspread, and a bulletin board beside the small desk was papered with pictures of dresses and blouses cut out from magazines and photos of flowers. A photo of solemn man with gray hair and a thick mustache was carefully pinned in the very middle. Melody leaned in to look at it. "Is that your dad?"

Leah picked at a thread on the bedspread. "Um, no. He died when I was a baby. That's his dad, my *zayde*."

Melody's confusion must have shown on her

face, because Leah supplied, "My grandfather."

"Is Zayde his name?" Melody asked.

"His name is Samuel," Leah replied. "Zayde is what I call him. It means 'grandfather' in Yiddish. What do you call your grandfather?"

"Poppa," Melody said.

Leah laughed. "See, I'd think that was your dad." She pointed at the photo. "This is Zayde in Krakow, before the war. One of my aunts found it and sent it to us a few years ago. We'd never seen a picture of him from that time—everything was destroyed in the war. Everything. Even—" Leah's voice caught.

Melody leaned forward. Maybe this was it, her chance to find out the secret of Leah's grandfather. The funny looks on her face, almost like she was hiding something. The way she sometimes seemed to stop herself talking, as if she was saying too much. "Even what?" Melody whispered.

"Nothing." Leah got up. "Here, come on."

Melody followed her back toward the kitchen, now deserted except for the stew bubbling merrily on the stove. Leah opened a door near the refrigerator that led down another narrow, dark hallway to a door at the end.

"Back when this house was first built, this was the maid's room," Leah explained. "That's why it's off the kitchen." She knocked softly on the closed door. "It's me."

"Come in, Leah-leh," a quavery voice called.

Leah opened the door, and Melody, her heart beating a little faster, entered the small room. A slight, gray-haired man, almost swallowed up by a large armchair, sat near the window reading a newspaper. Melody recognized him immediately as the man from the photo, though now he had a beard as well as a mustache. His face lit up as the girls came in.

"Come here, my dear," he said to Leah, setting down the paper. Melody could make out the name of it: *The Forward.* The rest of the paper was written in letters like the ones on Leah's refrigerator. Hazy sunlight filtered through the dusty window, and piles of books and papers stood everywhere— stacked by the armchair, heaped on the bedside table, covering the old-fashioned rolltop desk.

Leah went over and kissed his cheek. "This is my new friend, Melody. Melody, this is my grandfather, Dr. Roth."

"Delighted to meet you, Melody," Dr. Roth said. "What a pretty name." He spoke with a faint accent that made his *w*'s sound like *v*'s. He extended his hand and tried to rise from the chair, but a spasm of coughing overcame him and he fell back against the cushions, his cheeks an alarming shade of pale blue.

"Zayde!" Leah cried, rushing over to her grandfather. "Now sit still. Have you been overdoing again?" She grabbed a plaid blanket folded at the end of the bed and tucked it over his knees. Dr. Roth took a sip of water from a glass at his elbow and leaned his head against the back of the chair.

"Now, now, no fussing," he said after a moment. "See, I'm already better." The color had returned to his cheeks.

"No, you're not!" Leah said. "Now, sit there and don't try to get up again. Talk to Melody while I go make you a cup of tea." Against Dr. Roth's protests, Leah darted out of the room, leaving the door ajar behind her.

"Now, dear, come here and tell me about yourself," Dr. Roth said before Melody had a chance to feel awkward. He pointed to a footstool, and Melody perched on it.

"Um, well, I'm ten. I live in the next neighborhood over, about nine blocks from here. Leah and I met at the Fair Housing picnic."

Suddenly a glow of green and coral and violet caught her eye. A slender plant stood on an ornately carved plant stand beside the window. Its coral and violet blossoms glowed like jewels in the dimness of the room, and the long, thick leaves spread broad and smooth and as green as jade. But most amazing of all were the purple petals that curled and cascaded down from the blossoms like ribbons, hanging almost to the floor.

Melody inhaled. "Your plant is so beautiful!" she exclaimed, forgetting to feel shy. "Is it an orchid?"

Dr. Roth's face lit up again. "It is indeed! It is a lady's slipper orchid—one of the rarest orchids in the world. And one of the most beautiful. Its Latin name is *Paphiopedilum sanderianum*." He said the name as if it were a delicious candy he was eating.

Dr. Roth hoisted himself from his chair, leaning heavily on a cane, and shakily made his way over to the plant stand. He and Melody stood in front of the orchid in reverent silence. Melody felt almost as if she were at church, worshipping. The orchid was that beautiful.

"You see, my dear, how the petals curl as they

descend?" Dr. Roth pointed with a pencil. His voice was hushed. "That is the unique characteristic of this orchid. It is the only flower to do so and part of the source of its value."

"It's the loveliest flower I've ever seen," Melody said, as the door opened and Leah bustled in, carefully balancing a steaming cup of tea.

"Here, sit down," Leah fussed. "He won't take care of himself," she said to Melody. "And he needs to. His—"

"That's enough, Leah-leh," Dr. Roth cut in. "I'm fine, my dear. I was just discussing the lady's slipper orchid with Melody."

"He brought it from Poland," Leah told Melody. "The city of Krakow was falling to the Nazis. The university was shut down. People were starving in the streets."

"Your father was already here, thank God," Dr. Roth said. "I'd sent him and your grandmother once the troubles started. But . . . I thought I had more time." His voice dropped. His eyes gazed across the room, but Melody could tell they were seeing a different place, a different time. "They marched in the streets in perfect formation. We all watched. They ransacked the university. The greenhouses. All my beautiful orchids, my cuttings, my rare succulents. Gone. Tossed in a trash heap. Burned." The old man's voice caught.

Melody looked at Leah and saw the pained look on her face again. Was this the secret she was keeping? Her grandfather's dark past?

Dr. Roth cleared his throat and went on, more strongly. "The city was under siege. We were taken from our homes with guns at our backs. We were moved into the ghetto. We wore the clothes we were taken in until they were rags. We ate what we found in the gutters. But I kept my rarest orchid safe. It came with me on the ship to America. It was just a cutting then, so it did not have blossoms to be destroyed. I always kept it wrapped in a damp

rag, moist and warm. Orchids must have warmth."
He paused. The room was very quiet. Somewhere
Melody could hear a clock ticking. Her eyes were
fixed on Dr. Roth's face, as if under a spell.

"My friend Norman Muntz helped me get
passage to America. He told me which official to
bribe. I sold my father's watch—the last object of
his I had. All during the ocean journey, I kept the
orchid safe. I took it out on the deck so it could get
sun. I protected it from the salt spray. I found my
way to Detroit, to your father and grandmother.
Then I potted the orchid cutting, praying that it had
survived the voyage. It was the only thing I brought
with me from Poland besides the clothes on my
back. The cutting slowly took root and has thrived
ever since."

Dr. Roth fell silent again, staring through the
window, harsh lines cut into his gentle face. Melody
suddenly thought of Poppa's face last summer, as
he stood gazing at the land that had been his farm

in Alabama. He'd scooped up the dirt and let it run through his fingers, and he'd looked just like that.

"My grandpa had to leave his home, too," Melody said, surprising herself. She normally didn't go around telling people about her family's history, especially white people, but it just felt right all of a sudden. "They had a farm down South, and they sold the land so they could have a better life up here. But Poppa—that's my grandfather—didn't want to leave his farm."

Dr. Roth nodded and leaned forward. He placed his hand gently over Melody's. "He wanted to stay on the land he loved, didn't he?" Dr. Roth said. "His fatherland. It was the same with me."

"It *is* sort of the same, isn't it?" Melody said thoughtfully. "The Jews in Poland had to leave their homes, even when they didn't want to go. People who didn't like them just because of their race and religion drove them out. People who would hurt them—even kill them—if they stayed. That happened here in America, to people in my family." She thought again of what Val had said about Birmingham, and of the church there that was bombed last year. She and Leah really weren't so different.

"Except that we're working to make things better here," Leah said vigorously. She smiled at Melody.

"Now, did my two little flower lovers know there is to be a flower show at the Belle Isle Conservatory?" Dr. Roth asked.

"Yes! I'm going to help my grandfather," Melody volunteered. "Frank Porter. His flower shop is called Frank's Flowers."

"Your grandfather owns Frank's Flowers?" Dr. Roth asked. "I've stopped in that store once or twice, although it was years ago, before I cut back on my walking."

"You'll be back to it soon!" Leah said firmly. "I know you will."

How can she know that? Melody wondered. But

then, Leah did seem very sure of herself.

"Well then, I will see you at the flower show, Melody. I will be giving a talk on rare orchids at the Saturday Night Soiree. David Whitelaw, the head botanist, has invited me."

"I'm going to come and listen to his talk," said Leah. "So I'll see you there, too." The girls smiled at each other.

When it was time for Melody to leave, the girls said good-bye to Dr. Roth and made their way out of the apartment. On the sidewalk in front of the building, Leah faced Melody. "See how bad he is?"

"He doesn't seem real strong," Melody admitted. "I—I'm glad that you told me your grandfather's story. It must be hard to share it." She paused. "You know, you can tell me if you have a secret. I'd tell you if I had one. We don't have to hide things from each other."

Leah looked long at Melody and nodded slowly. Then she said softly, "There is something more."

Leaning against the crumbly brick wall of the apartment building, Leah said quietly, "He's sick. His heart is weak. He starved in the ghetto for years, and it permanently damaged his heart. That's why he gets out of breath. He's only sixty-eight, but he'll die soon if he doesn't get treated." Suddenly her voice broke. "And it's all their fault!"

"Whose fault?" Melody asked gently.

Leah's face was contorted with pain. "The Nazis! *They* destroyed his beautiful plants and stole his house, and *they* ruined his health. They didn't kill him back then, but they're doing it now." Leah stopped, struggling to control herself. Melody waited, tears stinging her own eyes.

At last, Leah went on. "But he's going to get better. I'm making sure of that. You see—" her voice dropped to a whisper—"there's a specialist in New York who treats cases like Zayde's. I'm going to fly him there, and he's going to get better."

"Wouldn't that be kind of expensive? To go to

New York on an airplane and everything?" Melody thought of the cramped apartment they'd just left. The Roths didn't seem like they had money to go jetting off to specialists in New York City. "Couldn't he just go somewhere here in Detroit?"

"No." Leah's voice was definite. "The only doctor who treats this kind of condition is in New York City. I read about it in a magazine." Her voice faltered and Melody shot her a quick glance, but then she went on. "That's why I babysit for the Myers. I'm saving my money for his plane ticket."

Leah was quiet a moment, her mouth flattened into that tense line, her eyes huge and watery. The tears spilled down her cheeks. "But he says he won't go," she whispered, and her face crumpled.

"What? What do you mean?" Melody put her arm across Leah's shoulder.

"It's not just the plane ticket—the treatment is a lot of money, too, and Zayde is refusing to get it." Leah began to weep softly.

Melody's heart ached with sympathy. She knew what grief felt like. She patted Leah's shoulder, trying to think of what to say. She remembered the days and weeks after the Birmingham church bombing. Four little girls had died, and Melody had felt deeply sad and frightened, too. Her heart had hurt, the way Leah's was hurting now.

She gave Leah's shoulder a squeeze. "My grand-mother told me we have to stand up to wrong, even when we hurt. We have to keep our hearts strong."

Leah was still a moment, as if she was thinking. Then she nodded slowly. "Keep your heart strong— I like that. Your grandmother sounds very wise." Sniffling, Leah rummaged in her dress pocket for a handkerchief.

"Here." Melody handed her her own. Poppa's face swam up again in Melody's mind. She tried to picture him weak and coughing, tried to picture knowing that he could be saved if he just got the right treatment. "You know, if it were my grandfather, I would do the same thing," she confided to Leah.

"You would?" Leah handed the hanky back, now damp and wrinkled. They started walking.

"Yes. I'd do anything for Poppa," Melody said.

"Really?" Leah sounded almost relieved. For a split second, Melody wondered why.

"Oh yes," Melody replied as they approached 12th Street.

Leah's face was calm now but determined. "Me too," she said. "Anything." She gave Melody a quick hug, then turned and walked back down the street toward her neighborhood.

Melody opened her front door. "Hi!" she called as she kicked off her sneakers. Mommy appeared in the doorway from the kitchen, still in her school-teacher clothes.

"Melody, honey, Val has called twice. You're supposed to be at Big Momma's, making brownies.

She's waiting for you. Did you forget?"

Melody's stomach plunged. "Oh shoot, yes. I did. I just got all caught up talking to Leah." Now she'd really done it. Val would be so mad. "Here, I'll call her. Can you drive me over, Mommy?"

Her mother shook her head. "It's too late now. I have to start dinner. You can just explain to Val and apologize."

Melody nodded, her stomach still swimming somewhere around her toes. She dialed. Big Momma answered on the third ring. "Melody, dear, we've missed you," she said once Melody said hello.

"I'm so sorry, Big Momma." Melody thought she'd never felt so guilty. "I was just all caught up talking to my friend Leah—"

"Well, it's not me you need to apologize to," Big Momma said. "Val's just putting the brownies in the oven. Hold on."

Melody gripped the receiver in a suddenly sweaty hand and listened to the murmur of voices on the other end. Then Big Momma came back on the line. "She's not coming to the phone, baby. Says she just wants to go home. You girls talk tomorrow and make up, hear?"

"Okay," Melody whispered and slowly put the receiver back on the cradle. Somehow, she didn't think making up would be as easy as Big Momma made it sound.

chapter 5

Secrets for Two

DING-DING! THE BELL over the door of
Poppa's flower shop tinkled as Melody pushed
open the glass door the next day. The little shop felt
as familiar to her as her own bedroom. Gray and
black linoleum covered the floor, and the high front
counter ran the length of the room, wood-paneled
and glossy. Along one wall, big refrigerator cases
held bouquets and arrangements. There were vases
of baby pink roses, some big sprays of purple irises,
and chrysanthemums—Melody's favorite.

The air was cool and a little damp and smelled
of potting soil, pine-scented floor cleaner, and a
spicy smell that came from the big pail of dried
eucalyptus branches that always stood at the side of
the counter.

Poppa was ringing up a woman with a bob hairdo, so Melody straightened the rack of ribbons while she waited. "There you go, Mrs. Davis," Poppa said, shutting the cash register drawer and sliding a tissue-paper-wrapped bouquet of yellow mums across the counter. "I think your mother will love those. Be sure to tell her to clip the ends before she puts them in water."

"Thank you, Mr. Porter," Mrs. Davis said, passing Melody in a puff of violet perfume. The door tinkled again, and Poppa turned to Melody with a big smile.

"Now, who is this? My new employee?"

"Very funny, Poppa," Melody laughed. "You know I'm here to help you get the plants ready for the Belle Isle flower show. Guess what? I met someone who knows you! His name is Dr. Roth—he's a botany professor—or at least he was—and he says he's come in here before. And he has this orchid with long blossoms that go almost to the floor! It's called a lady's slipper."

Poppa took a sip from his coffee mug near the cash register. "Samuel Roth? I do remember him. He stopped in a couple of times a while back. Nice man. And he has a lady's slipper orchid? Now that's special." Poppa came around the counter. "Let's get you started. We've got a lot to do for the flower show. Come on, I'll show you where I have everything laid out."

Melody followed Poppa into his workroom, her favorite place in the world. The big wooden work table stood against one wall, and sunlight poured from the windows. High metal shelves lined the other walls from floor to ceiling on both sides. They held everything you could want for arranging and potting flowers: baskets, clear and colored glass vases, green foam florist blocks, green tissue paper, white tissue paper, white cotton string, brown hemp twine, raffia twine, terra-cotta pots, potting soil, fertilizer, fungus killer, white cardboard boxes, and rows of ribbon in every color.

Poppa had already set out big pots of daffodils and irises on the table. "Our display is going to have the best potted flowers from the shop, as I told you the other day," Poppa explained. "We need to get some ribbons on these pots and get them boxed up nicely. You think you can do that?"

"Yes, Poppa," Melody told him. "They'll be the prettiest pots the flower show has ever seen."

"I knew you could do it, Little One." Poppa smiled at Melody, as the bell tinkled again out front. "I'll go help that customer, but I'll come back and see how you're doing in a few minutes."

Alone in the back, Melody turned on the dusty black radio and hummed along to "My Guy" as she clipped off some lengths of lavender ribbon. The song made her think of her brother, Dwayne, who was singing for Motown Records.

A shadow in the doorway made Melody look up. Val stood there, holding another box of daffodils. "Hey," Melody said, watching Val carefully as her cousin set the box down on the table. Had Val forgiven her for forgetting the brownie date?

"Hey," Val said briefly. She started lifting the daffodils from the box. "I came by to help Poppa. He brought this box from home."

"Okay, great! We really need some more help!" Melody knew she sounded overenthusiastic, but she wanted the awful distance to be gone from Val's voice.

A silence stretched out as the girls cut and tied ribbons. Val made a few fancy bows. The only sounds were the radio in the background and the snip of their scissors. Finally, Melody couldn't stand it anymore.

"Listen, Val, I messed up the other day. I'm so sorry I forgot about brownies. I—I just stayed longer at Leah's than I expected. We got to talking, and . . ." Melody trailed off. She wanted to tell Val about Dr. Roth's past and the things that Leah had shared with her so that Val would understand why

Melody couldn't have just hurried away. But she knew Leah considered her grandfather's painful past a private matter, so it would be wrong to talk about it, even to Val.

"I figured that was what happened." Val's voice was cold. She kept her eyes on a double bow she was tying.

"I'm really sorry. It's just that—well, I couldn't just walk out on Leah." *Okay, maybe I did forget, but Val should be more understanding,* Melody told herself fiercely as she lined up the decorated iris pots in their cardboard box, turning each pot so that it fit perfectly against the others. She could feel Val watching her. Finally, reluctantly, she looked up. "What?"

"There's something you're not telling me, isn't there?" Val asked quietly. "Some secret the two of you have."

"No! No, of course not." Melody's voice sounded false even to her, and she felt awful. She and Val had always shared everything. But not this. She couldn't betray Leah's confidence.

"Well, fine. I hope you two have a great time telling secrets together." Val dropped her trowel on the table and flounced out of the room. A moment later, Melody heard the bell tinkle again.

Melody stood alone, taking deep breaths, wondering if she was going to cry. She felt as if she'd done something terrible, but what could be so terrible about keeping Leah's secrets? Leah had confided in her alone, Melody argued with herself. Surely Leah didn't want Melody to blab about her grandfather all over the place. Melody picked up the box of daffodils. Val was just being oversensitive. She would get over it.

One thing was for sure—Melody wasn't going to give up Leah's friendship or break her trust. Leah didn't seem to have anyone else to talk to. *Leah needed her.*

chapter 6

Prepping for the Big Day

FRIDAY AFTER SCHOOL, Poppa pulled up in front of the conservatory and set the brake on the truck. "Here we are!"

Melody hopped out and trotted around to the back of the truck, where Poppa was already pulling out cardboard boxes of potted bulbs. The air was warm, and a stiff breeze was blowing off the river. To Melody, it smelled like adventure. Station wagons and vans were lined up along the gravel drive outside the conservatory, and the big metal-and-glass front doors were propped open. Two men in overalls were up on ladders, hanging a banner that read:

Belle Isle Conservatory Flower Show
Sponsored by the Detroit Metro Flower Fanciers

A smaller sign was posted below on the door: *Flower Show Preparations in Progress. Public Not Admitted.* People went in and out of the doors, pulling wagons of plants and carrying folded tables and large pieces of painted plywood that Melody guessed were parts of booths.

Carrying a box of irises, Melody followed Poppa up the wide cement steps toward the huge glass dome. Something brushed her head as she passed through the door, and she looked up.

"Sorry, little girl," one of the workmen called as he pulled up the drooping banner. "Guess we need to hang that a little higher."

Melody smiled at him, and then caught her breath as she stepped into the rotunda. She'd visited once before on a school field trip, but this time was even more thrilling. Maybe it was the sun streaming in through the dome or the busy bustle inside. Or maybe it was having Poppa by her side and the excitement of the flower show approaching.

The massive glass dome soared a hundred feet above her, spreading its huge metal arches over the palm fronds that seemed almost as high. Flowering trees nodded their lacy heads, while azaleas and wisteria draped gracefully over boulders, as sweet and languid as ladies lying down for a nap. Leaves and blossoms massed themselves wherever she turned, and the air was damp, sweet with blossom scent and musical with distant running water. It felt like a tropical fairyland in the middle of Detroit.

"You see that vine?" Poppa pointed to a trellis supporting a vine with blue flowers. "That's called Queen's Wreath. It's native to the Caribbean. This is one of the oldest ones in North America. And look at that passionflower! Ever see a prettier shade of purple?

"It's beautiful," Melody breathed, staring at the complicated, fuzzy blossom.

Staff members in green smocks rushed about. Exhibitors were scattered around the rotunda tacking up signs and arranging pots of plants. Melody saw one small bald man fussing over a row of African violets, misting them with a small sprayer. A large woman with a wildly flowered dress and glasses swinging from a chain was holding one end of a plywood slab and issuing directions at a man in overalls who was on his knees, busily hammering. Melody couldn't help noticing that she and Poppa were the only black people. She glanced up at Poppa, but he didn't seem to notice.

"Now, let's find our booth spot," he said, scanning the area, balancing the box of daffodils he carried.

A thin woman wearing a green smock and her gray hair in a bun bustled over to them, holding a clipboard. "Yes?" she asked officiously. "Making a delivery?"

Melody flushed. The woman thought Poppa was a deliveryman!

But Poppa didn't seem upset. "No, I'm an exhibitor. Frank's Flowers," he said.

"Oh! I see." She scanned her list. "Ah yes, here you are. Booth number forty-two." She pointed with a pen to an empty booth about halfway down the rotunda.

"Poppa, she thought you were a deliveryman," Melody whispered as they made their way down the row.

"I know, Little One." Poppa smiled down at her. "Some people are so used to thinking one way, it's hard for them to change," he said. "You got to just let some things roll off your back." He scanned the empty booth. "Now, let's get to work!"

Half an hour later, Melody stood back, hands on her hips, and surveyed the booth. Poppa's white, pink, and green banner was strung proudly across the top: *Frank's Flowers: Greening Detroit*, it read.

Poppa straightened up and mopped his fore-head with a big white handkerchief and then sat down on a folding chair and unpacked a thermos of iced tea. "Do you want some, or do you want to go look around?" he asked Melody.

"Can I look around, Poppa?" Melody asked. She was itching to see what the other exhibitors were showing.

"Go on, go on," Poppa waved his hand. "You go see what you can see."

The booths were arranged in a circle around the massive rotunda—probably fifty in all, with every type and shape of plant and flower, from cactuses to ferns. Melody started walking slowly around the circle, her hands clasped behind her back, just drinking in the air redolent of soil and leaves. Not far from Poppa's booth, the large woman she'd noticed earlier was bending over a tray of spiky plants with shiny leaves. Her pink-flowered dress reminded Melody of Big Momma's shower curtain. She was doing something with a pair of tweezers, but she straightened up when she saw Melody.

"Hi there!" she shouted in a raspy voice, though Melody was standing only a few feet away. "Come to see my babies? Aren't they gorgeous? Aren't you my little boo-boos?" she crooned at the plants.

Melody stopped, fascinated. Was she talking to the plants? Those were the little boo-boos? "What kind of plants are those?" Melody asked.

"These? These are exotics. See?" the woman pointed to a large, bright yellow banner. *Exotics by Vera* it blared in huge block letters. "That's me! I've been growing exotics for thirty years—cacti, succulents, bromeliads, Venus flytraps!" Her voice carried over the whole rotunda. Melody saw her neighbor on the other side, the bald man with the African violets, glance over and then shake his head.

"This is a jade vine!" Vera boomed. "Very rare, from the Philippines! I'm the only one here who has one!" Vera pointed to a vine hung thickly with striking blue-green flowers that dangled in long spiky clusters. Vera's eyes, small and glittering in her meaty face, peered out from behind thick glasses. "Now, these—these are the most special—" Suddenly she grabbed Melody by the wrist and dragged her behind the counter of the booth. Startled, Melody did not have time to resist. Vera, smelling of sweat and warm rose perfume, led Melody to a counter inside her booth. "My babies! My little precious darlings! The minute I saw these citron orchids at the Cleveland Flower Show, I knew I had to have them. You can't have a good collection of exotics without orchids—they're the belle of the ball!"

Vera bent over a row of small potted flowers. Melody knew they had to be orchids by their intricate, waxy blossoms and long, woody stems. These were a delicate yellow-white striped with green and had deep, pouchlike throats. "You are the most beautiful of all," Vera crooned. "Yes, now, Mommy's here. Wes. Wes she is. There now. Iss oo firsty? Does oo need a drinky? A drinky-poo?" With the utmost care,

Vera tilted a green plastic watering can over the pots.

Melody watched her, struggling to keep a straight face. The orchids were lovely, but did Vera always talk to her plants in baby talk? Melody knew you should never laugh at anyone. She bit her lip hard until the pain wiped away the impulse to giggle.

Vera seemed distracted by her orchids, so Melody edged away from her booth and continued on her circuit of the hall. She saw annuals and perennials, cut-flower bouquets, cacti and succulents, and potted bulbs like Poppa's. There were decorative grasses in huge pots and a collection of native plants that looked a lot like the ones growing in the vacant lot down the street from her house.

By the time Melody returned to Poppa's booth, she felt as if she'd seen every flower in the world.

"What did you see, Little One?" Poppa asked, looking up from arranging the irises. His booth was filled now with the potted bulbs Melody had decorated and bright bouquets arranged against the back wall. "Anything interesting?"

Melody told him about Vera and her orchids and all the rest of what she'd seen. "Our booth looks the best, Poppa," she told him. It really did. The flowers were bright shades of purple, white, and yellow, tall and strong, without a brown spot or a wilted leaf among them.

Poppa surveyed his flowers with pride. "Yes, these are beauties," he said. "Now, we have plenty of time. Let's go visit the orchid room. It's my favorite place in the conservatory, and I don't know if we'll have time to see it once the show starts. I'll show you some orchids that Miss Vera would give her right arm to have for her own."

chapter 7

In the Orchid Room

MELODY FOLLOWED POPPA out of the rotunda and down a short hallway. "We didn't get to go in the orchid room when our class was here. They said there were too many of us. I can't wait to see these orchids," Melody chattered as Poppa opened a set of doors. A billow of warm, damp air blew out as they entered, and Melody looked around with delight. Everywhere—sitting on little shelves, twisted on trellises, or hanging in woven baskets—orchids glowed, their bright blossoms like butterflies on slender, arching stems.

"This orchid collection is one of the best in the whole country," Poppa told Melody as they started walking slowly along the little stone path that wound through the room. "The collection came here during World War Two. You know that during the war in Europe, many valuable things were destroyed in the bombing?"

Melody nodded. Her big sister Lila, who was a bookworm, had once told her how the Germans had bombed the whole city of London in an action known as the Blitz. The thought of it gave Melody the chills, despite the warm, humid air.

"Well, a wealthy American woman from Detroit went to England at the start of the war and brought back some of that country's most valuable orchids to keep them safe. Later she donated them to the conservatory. So now those rare and valuable orchids are right here in Belle Isle," Poppa said, stopping by an orchid with wide, flat white petals. A pouch of petals at the bottom of the flower glowed purple. "These orchids are called *Paphiopedium delenatii* in Latin. They're very rare—worth a couple hundred dollars each."

"Really?" Melody examined the waxy flowers.

She knew from her book that orchids were rare and special, and she remembered Leah saying they were valuable, but she had no idea they could be worth *that* much. Melody thought fleetingly of Dr. Roth's orchid, wondering if it was worth as much as these—or more.

Poppa bent to examine the flower. "Now, Melody, do you see how the throat of this blossom is very deep?"

As Poppa spoke, the door to the room swung open, and a man rushed in. He wore a natty dark blue suit, and his slicked-down hair was combed with a part so sharp it looked as if it had been made with a ruler. Everything about him suggested order and precision.

"Excuse me! Excuse me! Just what do you think you're doing in here?" the man called as he hurried over. Melody noticed a gold name tag pinned to his lapel. *David Whitelaw,* it said. *Belle Isle Conservatory Manager and Senior Botanist.* Melody realized he must be the botanist that Dr. Roth had mentioned.

"I was just showing my granddaughter—" Poppa started to explain, but the man didn't seem to hear.

"The conservatory is not open for visitors right now," Mr. Whitelaw said, his eyes darting around rapidly. "I'm afraid I must ask you to leave."

Melody swallowed, remembering the time she and Dwayne had to leave Fieldston's Clothing Store because the manager thought they were shoplifting—just because they were black. She felt a pinch of the anger and humiliation that had engulfed her that day a year ago. Would Mr. Whitelaw be fussing like this if they were white? Somehow, Melody didn't think so.

Poppa straightened his back. "Mr. Whitelaw," he said with dignity. "We haven't been introduced. I am Frank Porter. I own Frank's Flowers, and I have a booth here at the flower show." Poppa pointed to his apron, which had the shop's logo. Melody thought she could see Mr. Whitelaw relax slightly.

Poppa went on. "My granddaughter has never seen the conservatory's extraordinary orchid collection. She's a plant lover too, just like her grandpa."

Mr. Whitelaw looked at Melody. She tried her most winning smile, but he just frowned a little and pushed an orchid back from a shelf behind Melody as if he was afraid she'd knock it over. "Humph." Mr. Whitelaw cleared his throat. "Well, I suppose it's all right then," he said reluctantly. "But please be careful."

What does he think we're going to do? Melody wondered. *Knock a bunch of orchids over?* But she held her tongue as Mr. Whitelaw left, giving them one last backward glance over his shoulder.

"Come on, Little One," Poppa said. "Let's look at these. Have you seen the monkey face orchid?"

"Poppa," Melody murmured as she gazed at the little peach-colored flower Poppa pointed out. It did have markings that looked just like a monkey's face. "Do you think that manager was being so mean to us because we're the only black people here?"

Poppa looked over at Melody, then put both hands on her shoulders. "I don't know, baby. He might be a fussbudget with everyone right before a flower show. We have to stand up for ourselves, but we can't forget to be kind and respectful as well. Remember, Reverend King says, 'The ultimate measure of a man is not where he stands in moments of comfort and convenience, but where he stands at times of challenge and controversy.'"

The words flowed through Melody's veins like a bracing tonic. She nodded firmly and straightened her shoulders. Poppa was right. It was when things got difficult that you could really show what you were worth.

When they had admired all the orchids, Melody followed Poppa back into the main rotunda and over to their booth. As they passed the front doors, Melody saw Mr. Whitelaw talking to someone trying to enter. "The conservatory is closed for the

flower show setup," he was saying. "You'll have
to come back another time." Melody had to admit
that he sounded just as brusque to this red-haired
man as he had to her and Poppa. Maybe Poppa was
right, thought Melody; Mr. Whitelaw was just like
that—fussy and bossy. As the other man nodded
and left, Melody turned his face over in her mind
while she followed Poppa back to their booth. He
looked sort of familiar, but she couldn't think where
she had seen him before. Maybe he was one of
Poppa's customers, Melody thought as she retied a
ribbon that had gotten mussed in the moving.

A little while later, she heard another commotion near the front door and looked up. It was
Dr. Roth, making his way into the rotunda with his
cane. Leah supported his other elbow. She spotted
Melody and waved.

"Poppa, there's my new friend, Leah!" Melody
said. "And that's her grandpa, Dr. Roth."

"Well now, I'd like to meet them both," Poppa

said, setting down his watering can.

Melody led him over to the pair. "Leah, this is *my* zayde," she said, smiling. "Frank Porter."

Leah laughed. "It's nice to meet you, Mr. Porter. This is my *poppa*, Samuel Roth." Both girls giggled.

"Frank's Flowers?" Dr. Roth said. He held out his hand, and Poppa shook it. "I was telling your granddaughter that I used to stop in every now and then. It's a fine shop!" Dr. Roth was dressed up today in a brown three-piece suit—quite old looking but freshly ironed. His scanty white hair was carefully combed with Brylcreem. "Leah was good enough to introduce me to your granddaughter, Mr. Porter. We had a lovely chat about orchids."

Before Poppa could reply, a voice rang out across the rotunda. "My dear sir!" Mr. Whitclaw rushed across the stone floor like a bolt of navy blue lightning and pounced on Dr. Roth. "What an honor, a true honor!" he crooned, as the rest of the exhibitors stopped what they were doing and watched.

I guess he isn't snippy to everyone, after all, Melody thought.

"David, good afternoon," Dr. Roth greeted Mr. Whitelaw genially. "How is your collection coming along?" Dr. Roth turned to Poppa. "David himself is quite a collector of orchids."

"Oh, I'm just an amateur." Mr. Whitelaw waved his hand in the air as if brushing away invisible gnats. "Dr. Roth, we are all looking forward with great anticipation to your talk tomorrow at the Soiree."

Melody smiled at Leah as Mr. Whitelaw fawned over Dr. Roth, but Leah didn't smile back. Her eyes were darting around the rotunda, and she seemed preoccupied. Sweat beaded her upper lip, though they were standing in the cool breeze from the doors. *She must be nervous having her grandfather out with his ill health,* Melody decided.

Then, past Leah's shoulder, she noticed Vera. Vera was leaning over the front of her booth, craning her neck toward them to get a good look. She was going to pull her booth over with her if she didn't watch out. Melody stifled a giggle at the thought of Vera and the booth collapsing in a plywood-and-flowered-dress disaster.

"Some amateurs have amassed superb collections," Dr. Roth was saying when Melody tuned back into the group. "Now, I was reading recently that collectors are finding some unusual orchids in Central America—Guatemala, specifically, I believe. Very interesting. Some species are brand new to us here in the United States."

"Oh! Oh." Mr. Whitelaw's mouth twitched. "Yes. Interesting. Very interesting." He pressed his lips together. There was a long pause as everyone looked at him. Melody noticed his hands were trembling. "I'm sorry. I need to check on . . . to make a phone call. The *Detroit News* is doing a story . . ." He rushed away toward the back of the rotunda.

Everyone stood in surprised silence. "Well!" said Dr. Roth. "Leah, dear . . . Where did she go?"

Melody looked around. Leah wasn't standing with them.

"Do you know where she went, my dear?" Dr. Roth asked Melody.

"I don't know, Dr. Roth. Should I look for her?" Melody said.

"Yes, please, if you would. I'll just sit on this bench and wait for her." He lowered himself slowly to the padded bench.

Melody wandered toward the gift shop and poked her head in. The lights were off in the tiny space. "Leah?" she called. There was no answer. A short hallway lined with doors extended off the back of the rotunda. Melody pushed open the green door to the ladies room. "Leah? Your grandpa's waiting," she called into the tiled interior. It was deserted—no feet were visible below the stalls.

Melody withdrew and started back to the

rotunda. She heard footsteps behind her and turned. Leah was walking quickly toward the rotunda also.

"Oh, there you are!" Melody said. "I was just looking for you. Where were you?"

"Um, just getting some fresh air," Leah said, swiping at her hair, which was a little disheveled. A bright spot of color burned high on each cheek. "You know . . . it's so hot in here."

Actually, the air was delightfully cool and damp, thought Melody, but she didn't point that out. She looked closer at her friend. "You look kind of funny," she said. "Are you getting sick? Maybe that's why you feel hot—you're getting a fever."

"Yes, that's probably it," Leah said quickly. "Come on, let's get back." She walked rapidly down the hallway, and Melody had to struggle to keep up.

Melody lay in bed that night, staring at the wall. Her nightgown was twisted around her body, and the sheets were rumpled. Across the room, her sister Lila breathed steadily and slowly. But sleep would not come to Melody. All the excitement of the afternoon kept flipping through her mind. In the morning, she and Poppa would go back to the conservatory for the opening of the flower show. Then tomorrow night was the Saturday Night Soiree. Melody flopped over on her side and stared at her clock. Eleven thirty.

"You still awake, honey?" Mommy stood silhouetted in the doorway, the hall light yellow behind her.

"Yes," Melody whispered. "I can't sleep."

The bed creaked as Mommy sat down on the edge. She smoothed Melody's hair back with her cool hand. "You had a big day today, and you've got a bigger one tomorrow. How was it at the conservatory? You were awfully quiet at dinner."

Melody sighed and turned onto her back. She stared at the milky-glass light fixture. "It was beautiful. I saw all these special plants. But there was this man, the manager . . ." She told her mother about Mr. Whitelaw scolding Poppa and her in the orchid room. "He was really mean. I wondered if . . . well, you know, we're the only black people exhibiting at the show. The way that man talked to us—well, it made me think of that time with Dwayne and me at Fieldston's."

Mommy tucked the coverlet up around Melody's shoulders. "Of course, you always have to be careful. People do watch us more closely sometimes, and when we see unfairness, we have to stand up to it when we can. You've always done your part. Remember when you closed your account at the bank after they wouldn't hire Yvonne just because she's black? You have to choose your moment, that's all. It sounds like this Mr. Whitelaw is probably just a fussy kind of person. Didn't you say he was rude to someone else, too?"

"Yes, a man who was trying to get in, and he was white." Melody thought back to the moment, the man trying to enter as she and Poppa were walking back to their booth from the orchid room. He had red hair. . . . Suddenly, she remembered why his face looked vaguely familiar: He was the same man she'd seen outside the conservatory the day she'd gotten separated from Val and Leah.

"Well, I wouldn't worry about him." Mommy patted Melody's knee through the covers. "You have bigger things to focus on—like making sure Poppa's booth is the most beautiful one at the show tomorrow. And don't forget the party tomorrow night!"

"Oh no, I won't forget that," Melody said.

Mommy straightened the sheets and kissed Melody on the forehead. Melody snuggled down under the cool sheets. She was ready for tomorrow.

chapter 8

An Accusation

"GOOD THING WE'RE here so early,
Poppa," Melody said happily the next morning as
Poppa held the big conservatory doors open for her.
"Don't you think we should water the irises before
the show opens? And Mommy packed us deviled
eggs for lunch! And strawberries—" She stopped.
"What's going on?"

The rotunda was full of booths overflowing with
flowers, just like yesterday—but many of the exhibitors were clustered in a little group, whispering.
Melody noticed Vera was not among them. She was
at her booth, bent over her orchids again. Melody
could see her lips moving as she whispered to them.

The conservatory staff in their green smocks
were rushing here and there with worried looks on

their faces. Suddenly Melody caught her breath. In one corner of the rotunda, Mr. Whitelaw was standing with two policemen.

"Poppa! Look!" she whispered, tugging on her grandfather's arm. Mr. Whitelaw was talking rapidly, his face creased with anxiety as one of the officers, a young, tall man with a crew cut, took notes. The other one, rounder and older with a red face and glasses, surveyed the room, his thumbs hooked into his belt.

Poppa shook his head. "Come on, Little One. This doesn't concern us. Let's see how our flowers did overnight."

Melody trailed Poppa to the booth, watching the policemen out of the corner of her eye. Was it her imagination, or was Mr. Whitelaw looking at Poppa? The young policeman nodded at something the botanist was saying, and then he looked around, and Melody felt his gaze come to rest on her. Quickly, she ducked her head and focused on filling the watering can from the spigot next to their booth.

"What do you think is going on, Poppa?" she whispered.

Poppa was going over a clipboard, his glasses pushed onto his forehead. He shook his head. "Don't know. I expect we'll find out shortly. Just focus on your work."

Melody concentrated on watering the irises, but she watched the policemen, too. They were drawing closer. *What in the world?* Melody burned with curiosity. What could have happened to bring the police to a flower show of all places?

Suddenly, the young policeman loomed over their booth. *Officer Baer,* his name tag read. Mr. Whitelaw was at his elbow, looking distinctly less polished than yesterday. His thinning brown hair hung in wisps over his forehead, and his hands were shaking. Melody noticed large sweat stains spreading under the arms on his shirt.

"This—this is the, ah—person I mentioned to you," Mr. Whitelaw said to the police officer.

Poppa looked up from his clipboard in surprise. Melody put down the watering can.

"Mr.—" Officer Baer consulted his notepad. "Mr. Porter, we'd like to ask you a few questions."

"Me?" Poppa asked. "What's this all about?" He looked at Mr. Whitelaw.

"There was a theft here last night," Mr. Whitelaw declared heatedly. "Five of the rarest orchids from the orchid room, stolen!"

Melody gasped.

"Sir," the officer said to Poppa, "Where were you last evening at five-thirty?"

"Me?" Poppa looked from Mr. Whitelaw to the officer, bewildered. "Where? . . . I was right here, setting up my booth."

The full implication of the officer's question dawned on Melody. She could see Poppa realizing it at the same time.

"I *caught* you two in the orchid room!" said Mr. Whitelaw, pointing a trembling finger at Poppa. "You were meddling with the *delenatii* orchids!"

"What?" Poppa said. "No—I was showing the orchids to my granddaughter." He gripped the edge of the counter and looked from Mr. Whitelaw to Officer Baer. For the first time, thought Melody, Poppa looked scared.

Melody thought she was going to choke. Was the conservatory manager really saying that *Poppa* stole the orchids? Her gentle Poppa, who loved flowers, accused of *stealing* them? Bile rose in Melody's throat, and her heart pounded. Anger and fear filled her until she saw swirls of red in front of her eyes.

Officer Baer looked at Poppa sternly. "Sir, you are in the flower trade?"

"Of course he is," Melody cried. "He's the owner of Frank's Flowers on 12th Street. He's been in the flower business for years!"

The three men looked at her. "Shh, baby," Poppa whispered.

"Sir, we're going to have to ask you to step out of your booth for some further questions," said Officer Baer. He flipped his notepad closed and slid it into his breast pocket.

Melody's stomach plunged as if she were flying down a roller coaster hill. Were they saying that Poppa might be charged with the theft? She glanced at him in horror.

Poppa's face had turned ashy, and he sat down suddenly on the folding chair.

Mr. Whitelaw nodded rapidly, as if agreeing with Officer Baer. Melody wanted to push him over. She clenched her fists and stared at Mr. Whitelaw.

"Right now? Poppa asked quietly. "Am I being charged with a crime, Officer?" The clipboard trembled in his fingers.

"No one's being charged with anything . . . yet,"

Officer Baer replied. "If you'll just come with us."

"I'm here with my granddaughter," Poppa said. Melody could hear a small shake in his voice. "I can't leave her."

"I'll be all right, Poppa," Melody whispered. She could hardly believe what was happening. One minute they were watering plants, and the next minute Poppa was being taken away for questioning.

"We'll just talk in a back office right here in the building," Officer Baer said laconically. "It won't take long."

Poppa swallowed and nodded. He put his hands on Melody's shoulders and leaned in close to her. "Now you stay calm, Little One. Watch over the booth. And don't worry about me. I'll be back before you know it."

Tears suddenly prickled Melody's eyes, but she blinked them back hard. Poppa didn't need to worry about her, too.

"I'll be fine," she said, trying to sound brave.

Poppa squeezed Melody's shoulder. The touch of his big, rough hand felt as familiar as the sight of his face. She grabbed his hand from her shoulder and squeezed it tight, wishing she could hold on to it forever. Officer Baer started moving away. Gently, Poppa pulled his hand from Melody's grasp. She squeezed her eyes shut. She didn't want to see him leaving the rotunda with the police.

chapter 9

Presumed Guilty

THERE WAS ONLY an hour until the show opened and the public started streaming in. Melody sat still on her chair and tried to process what had happened. Poppa hadn't done anything—surely he couldn't be accused of this crime!

But a nagging feeling told her that he could. He could be presumed guilty unless proven innocent— just like yesterday in the orchid room, and just like that day at Fieldston's Clothing Store.

Melody sprang up from her chair. She couldn't just sit here. Poppa had said to watch over the booth, but this was her only chance to see if she could find out anything about the theft. She knew beyond the shadow of a doubt that Poppa hadn't taken the orchids, but maybe if she looked around, she could learn something about whoever *had.*

Snoop around, Melody told herself. *See if you can pick up any gossip about the theft.*

It wasn't hard. At every booth Melody passed, the exhibitors were buzzing.

". . . came in and found them missing from the orchid room," one exhibitor was saying to another as Melody pretended to tie her shoe in front of their booths.

". . . took the *delenatii* orchids—the rarest ones in the conservatory!" a man was telling a well-dressed woman who took deep drags on a cigarette. "Worth a lot of money. Whoever took them knew what they were doing."

Melody paused at Vera's booth. Vera liked to talk—and she loved orchids. "Can you believe this orchid theft?" Melody asked.

Vera's hair looked disheveled. "I most certainly cannot! A *terrible* thing! That someone would take those babies, so precious, so innocent . . ." She leaned close to Melody. "And *do you know*—" she paused, giving Melody a stern look—"that our very own David Whitelaw was once accused of stealing orchids?"

"He was?" Melody couldn't hide her shock.

"Well, not exactly *stealing*. He just got into a bit of trouble, let's say." Vera opened her bleary eyes wide. "He's always been *obsessed* with orchids, just *crazy* about them. Did you know he was once married to my sister-in-law's niece? Anyway, about ten years ago, back when they were still married, he went off to Guatemala on a collecting trip. And my dear, he and his compatriots used some *very* unsavory practices to gather their specimens, really *criminal*, you know." Vera breathed hard. The odor of stale coffee wafted in Melody's face.

But Melody wanted to hear more. This could be important! "Like what?" she asked Vera.

"Like plucking rare orchids out of a tree by the roots. Some orchids grow in trees, and taking the roots means the orchid will never regrow there. Pillaging, let's just say. He was caught at customs trying to enter the U.S. with a suitcase full of specimens—some very rare orchids and other plants that he'd taken for his collection. *Terrible*, don't you think?"

"Oh yes, terrible," Melody managed as she slowly edged away. She perched on the low stone wall near the gift shop to think. So Mr. Whitelaw had stolen orchids before! Well, maybe not stolen, exactly, but taking plants that weren't his and treating them irresponsibly, just for his own personal collection. Melody couldn't help wondering: Could Mr. Whitelaw have chosen this moment—when there were plenty of other suspects about, with all the flower show exhibitors—to steal the conservatory's five rarest orchids?

Melody almost bounded up from the wall, feeling positive she had solved the crime, when a thought held her back: What about Vera herself?

She seemed awfully eager to implicate Mr. Whitelaw.
And she certainly loved orchids; she called them
her "precious darlings" and—Melody frowned,
trying to recall the details of that first odd conversation—oh yes, "the belle of the ball." Vera was
definitely an odd bird. Maybe she was spreading
gossip about Mr. Whitelaw to deflect attention from
herself.

Melody bit her lip, thinking hard. There was
something else Vera had said yesterday—"*When I
saw those orchids at the Cleveland Flower Show, I knew
I had to have them.*"

Did Vera want orchids badly enough to steal
them?

Melody scanned the rotunda. The doors were
open now, and the public was starting to filter in.
Poppa's booth would soon be crowded with flower
lovers. She had to work fast.

Melody wove her way among the booths as the
rotunda began filling with visitors. Spring jackets

and the backs of dresses loomed in front of Melody as she ducked through the crowd. The dull roar of conversation echoed off the high glass walls. Melody skirted the crowd, scanning faces and keeping her ears open.

"Oh, now these roses . . ."

"Just like my grandmother used to grow . . ."

"Mildred! You must see these begonias!"

Melody sighed as she waded through the masses of people. Women cooing over the flowers and men checking their watches. She should get back to the booth. If only Poppa were back! Briefly, she pictured Poppa sitting at a big metal table with a light shining on him, like in the movies. Two cops in front of him. *Admit you're the thief!* one of them yelled in Melody's mind. *Admit it!*

"*Oof!*" Melody ran into a shirtfront. "Sorry!" she gasped, looking up. A man in a tan fedora was standing over her, rubbing his stomach.

The man smiled at her in a friendly way. "No

harm done." His voice was a rich, deep baritone, like someone on the radio. He looked familiar— she thought he might be the same man she'd seen yesterday trying to come in despite the sign in front saying the conservatory was closed. Mr. Whitelaw had sent him away. That man had had red hair, and this man was wearing a fedora, so it was hard to be sure. But his voice—there was something about his voice that jogged her memory. She just couldn't place it. Melody looked up—the man was gone, vanished into the anonymous crowd all around her.

Suddenly it came to her, where she had heard that voice before: the day she had seen Leah in the alley arguing with a man! Melody had almost forgotten about that strange encounter. She felt quite certain it was him. What had he and Leah been arguing about? And why was he here now?

People pressed all around her. The air was growing hot and stuffy. Melody decided to step outside, just for a moment. She slipped through the crowd and pushed her way outside to the wide cement plaza, bathed in sunshine.

A taxi pulled up at the curb, and to Melody's joy, Leah stepped out! Then Leah opened the back door and helped her grandfather out, handing him his cane.

"Leah!" Melody called, waving. She hurried over. "Hello, Dr. Roth."

"Hi!" Leah greeted Melody with a big smile. "How are you?" She gave Melody a squeeze.

She seemed upbeat today, thought Melody. Whatever had been bothering her yesterday must be better now.

"Did you hear about the theft?" Melody asked them.

"We did. Such a distressing event," Dr. Roth said. "We've come out to offer the police and the conservatory whatever help we can."

Melody nodded, holding back sudden tears. "They took Poppa for questioning," she whispered, feeling ashamed, as if Poppa had done something wrong, even though she knew he hadn't.

"Oh, my dear." Dr. Roth patted her shoulder with a gnarled hand. "How distressing. You mustn't worry, though. Of course Mr. Porter knows nothing about this, as the officers will no doubt discover."

"Aren't they questioning everyone?" Leah asked.

"I don't think so. Just Poppa." Melody sniffled, and Dr. Roth offered her a folded white hanky. It smelled like Poppa's hankies, which made Melody feel a tiny bit better. She wiped her nose and eyes.

"There now! Shall we go inside?" Dr. Roth said bracingly. He hobbled toward the busy front entrance, where people were streaming in and out of the open front doors.

Leah put her arm around Melody and hugged her. "Hey . . . I can't believe they took your grandfather in." Her voice was husky. "That's terrible. I—I never thought something like that would happen."

Melody glanced up at Leah. She had looked

bright and happy a moment ago, and now her mouth was tight and her eyes shiny, almost as if she were about to cry, too. "What do you mean?" Melody asked her.

"Well, I—just that when I heard about the theft, I never thought your grandfather would be suspected . . ." Her voice trailed off. She looked miserable.

"Well, like your grandpa said, he'll be back soon." Melody spoke with a bravado she didn't feel.

Leah linked her arm with Melody's, and they walked toward the doors.

Inside, Dr. Roth was seated on the same cushioned bench as yesterday, with Mr. Whitelaw standing beside him.

"—so terribly, terribly sorry, Mr. Whitelaw," Dr. Roth was saying as Melody and Leah approached. "It is a sad crime, to steal flowers."

Leah made a little sound in her throat, but no one else seemed to hear. Melody wondered if she was feeling ill again, like yesterday.

Mr. Whitelaw had taken a handkerchief from his pocket and was twisting it in his sweaty hands. "And on the eve of the Soiree," he moaned. "And your talk, Dr. Roth! How will you discuss our rare and beautiful orchids with our donors when the five best specimens have been *stolen*?"

"Now, now," Dr. Roth soothed. "I was considering that problem during the cab ride over, and I have a solution to offer. I will bring my own lady's slipper orchid with me tonight and give a talk about it. The donors will be delighted, I predict."

Suddenly, a folding chair crashed to the floor with a clang. Everyone stared at Leah, who had fallen over along with the chair.

"Sorry," she whispered, extricating herself and setting the chair upright again. "Tripped."

Mr. Whitelaw looked at her with raised eyebrows, then turned back to her grandfather. "Oh, Dr. Roth, that would be very generous!" He clapped his hands together, looking as if he'd taken a tonic. "What a relief. Thank you, sir!" He glanced behind him. "Now, I see Officer Baer looking for me. I must attend to him. Please excuse me." He hurried away.

Poppa appeared beside Melody. "Here I am, Little One."

"Poppa!" Melody threw her arms around him and hugged him hard.

"There now," Dr. Roth exhaled, leaning back against the cushions of the bench. "Thank goodness you're back, Mr. Porter." His thin cheeks looked alarmingly pale, and his breath whistled when he spoke.

"Do you want some water, Dr. Roth?" Melody asked anxiously.

He shook his head. "Thank you, my dear. I just need a moment to collect myself."

Leah dropped down on the bench beside him and took his hand. "Zayde, I don't think you should bring the orchid here." Her voice was low and intense.

Dr. Roth blinked. "Why ever not?"

Leah swallowed and looked away. When she looked back, her face was calmer. "It's so valuable. What if *it* gets stolen, too? Or it could be damaged. Look at all these people—"

"Now my dear, we'll be very careful with it," Dr. Roth said soothingly. "David will have a separate stand for it, and we'll make sure it's roped off to keep the crowds back. You can be the bodyguard if you like." Dr. Roth smiled, but Leah did not. She gripped the fabric of her skirt in her fingers and looked up at Melody. Her eyes were large and round, like those of a rabbit caught in a trap.

chapter 10
What Will Happen to Poppa?

THE SMELL OF spaghetti sauce filled the house, competing with the scent of mown grass wafting in through the open windows. On the TV, the news competed with the clash of pans and cabinet doors from the kitchen. Big Momma and Poppa were coming over for dinner so Poppa and Melody could go to the Soiree. When he returned to the booth after being questioned by the police, Poppa hadn't said much about what had happened, and Melody didn't ask. His face looked so tired, though, and so old that her heart twisted just to look at him.

"Melody, honey, come in here and drain these noodles, please," Mommy called from the kitchen.

"Coming!" Melody called from the porch, where she had been sitting on the step with her chin in her hands, trying to sort through her thoughts. Would the Soiree even be any fun, with what had happened to Poppa that morning? Maybe they should just skip it, thought Melody. Then it occurred to her that the real thief might be there, hiding in plain sight—Mr. Whitelaw, or possibly Vera . . . and what about that man, that red-haired man who sometimes wore a tan fedora and who kept turning up at the conservatory . . . who was he, anyway?

And Val—Tish was dropping her off after dinner, so she could go with Poppa and Melody to the Soiree. Melody knew she couldn't let Val down again. And she was eager to tell Val what had happened and share her theories about it. Maybe Val could help her find information about the real thief tonight—that is, if her cousin wasn't still angry with her.

With a sigh, Melody realized that Leah would also be at the Soiree, since Dr. Roth was coming to give his lecture. Melody was interested to hear him talk about his orchid, but her stomach tightened at the thought of being with both Leah and Val at the party. Would Leah be feeling better? Would Val be standoffish? This morning Leah had seemed genuinely upset and concerned about the police questioning Poppa, and Melody knew Val would be upset as well. Leah and Val and she really had so much in common, Melody reflected. It should be easy for all three of them to be friends. But somehow, it wasn't.

Melody rose, still thinking, and made her way into the steamy kitchen, where Mommy was frying the last of the meatballs.

Mommy wiped her forehead with the back of her hand. "Lila, go fetch your Daddy, will you?"

Lila got up from kitchen table, where she was reading a thick book, and went out into the backyard, where Daddy had just finished mowing the grass.

Melody carefully poured the boiling water and noodles into the strainer, still thinking about the problem of being at the Soiree with both Leah and Val. All of a sudden, she didn't feel hungry anymore. She looked up to find Mommy watching her.

"What's on your mind?" her mother asked, forking the meatballs into a pot and mixing them with tomato sauce.

Melody half-smiled. She could never keep anything from Mommy. "Did Poppa tell you about—about the flower show?"

"Yes, Big Momma phoned me—" Mommy started to say, just as the timer on the stove beeped. Big Momma and Poppa came through the door at the same time, calling out greetings, and Daddy and Lila came in the back door. "We'll talk at dinner," Mommy said to Melody, taking rolls out of the oven. "Let's get this food on the table."

Melody hurried to her place at the table and joined hands with Lila and Daddy as Big Momma said grace.

"Amen," Big Momma finished, and everyone

started talking and passing around the dishes of spaghetti, salad, and rolls.

Poppa cleared his throat. "Folks, you know what happened this afternoon. This situation could affect us all if it gets any worse."

"How could they think you would steal orchids?" Melody burst out. "It's that Mr. Whitelaw! Just because he found us in the orchid room yesterday. And because—" *Because we're black,* she wanted to say.

Poppa sighed and pushed his glasses up on his forehead. He rubbed his eyes. "This is a shame, baby, it really is. It's also a shame those beautiful plants were stolen. Let's just hope whoever did this takes good care of them. But fretting won't bring those stolen orchids back."

"Daddy, this is serious," Mommy said, looking across the table with a worried frown. "If you're formally charged, there could be trouble."

Melody knew what Mommy meant. Poppa could be arrested. Even if he was proven innocent, it could ruin his reputation and his business. After all, who would buy flowers from someone accused of stealing them? And if Poppa had to pay for a lawyer to help him, that could get very expensive . . .

Melody's heart rose up in her throat, and she swallowed it back down as her eyes met Lila's across the table. She could read the fear in her sister's face that she knew was reflected in her own. Poppa couldn't lose his shop. Melody knew that Big Momma didn't charge much for the singing lessons she gave to kids in the neighborhood. Poppa's flower shop was what paid for their house and put food on their table. She knew that Poppa and Big Momma were also helping Yvonne pay her college tuition. If Poppa lost his flower shop, it would affect the entire family.

And he didn't do a thing, Melody shouted inside her head, *except exhibit at a flower show.*

chapter 11

The Soiree

BACK IN HER room after dinner, Melody took her freshly ironed pink-and-white polka-dot party dress from its hanger and buttoned it up the front. She was surprised to find that her fingers were trembling. She pulled on white, lace-trimmed bobby socks and stuffed her feet into her black patent-leather Mary Janes. She patted her hair, smoothing a few stray strands into her pink headband. Val would be here any minute.

The doorbell downstairs chimed, and Melody took a deep breath, trying to calm down.

"Hi," Val said as Melody opened the door. Val stood stiffly on the porch instead of bouncing inside as she usually did.

"You look so pretty!" Melody said as she took

Val's hand and pulled her cousin inside. Val's dress was cream-colored taffeta with a flounce around the bottom. "Did you hear about what happened to Poppa?"

Val nodded. "Yeah. Big Momma called." Her forehead was creased with anxiety.

"It's up to us to help him," Melody said quickly. She filled Val in on her suspicions about Vera and Mr. Whitelaw. "And this night is our last chance to get any more information on them," she finished. "So we have to watch them closely."

Val cleared her throat. "Will Leah be there?" She spoke delicately, as if anxious not to disturb the tentative peace between them.

"Yes—her grandfather's giving a talk. She can help us. I know she feels badly about Poppa, so she'll want to help," Melody said, hoping to soften Val's feelings toward Leah.

Poppa was putting on his evening jacket. In his stylish hat, bow tie, creased trousers, and shiny shoes, he no longer looked old and tired the way he had at dinner. In fact, thought Melody, he looked downright spiffy.

"Now, where are my dates?" he called, turning toward the girls. "Have you two lovely young ladies seen some little girls around here? They're supposed to come to a party with me tonight."

"Poppa, it's us! We're right here!" Melody and Val said, laughing. For the first time that night, Melody's heart lifted. It was so good to see some sparkle back in Poppa's eyes.

The night was warm and soft, with a gentle breeze off the river. The city lights glowed orange in the distance. They had left the asphalt and fumes of the city behind them. Out here on Belle Isle, the air was scented with wisteria, lilies, and the rising green, damp-earth fragrance of the spring soil.

Poppa held open the heavy metal-and-glass

door of the conservatory. "After you, ladies," he
said, grandly sweeping his arm inside. Melody
clutched Val's arm as they walked with Poppa into
the rotunda. The round glass dome was hung with
tiny white lights, twinkling like stars in among
the towering ferns and orange trees. Little tables
draped with white tablecloths were scattered
around, with candles flickering in the middle. In
one corner, a string quartet played bright classical
music. Ladies in silk dresses laughed with men in
dark suits. "Ooh," Melody breathed in awe.

"Wow, this is like a real grown-up party," Val
whispered. They were the only children there that
Melody could see. She looked around and spotted
Mr. Whitelaw almost immediately, circulating
through the crowd in a dark green suit and blue tie.
Then Melody saw the lady's slipper orchid, alone on
its own plant stand in the center of the rotunda. It
glowed under a special spotlight, its violet petals
cascading almost to the floor. Velvet ropes held

back the crowd that pressed around it, admiring
the spectacular blossoms. Mr. Whitelaw stood
nearby like a guard dog, chatting with a small knot
of elegantly dressed guests—the conservatory's
donors, Melody speculated. Vera was there, too,
dressed in a leopard-print dress and pink shoes.
Her glasses were askew, and she was pressing
against the ropes. Her eyes were fixed on the plant.
As Melody watched, riveted, Vera reached out a
finger to touch one of the long, curling petals. Mr.
Whitelaw immediately broke off his conversation
and shook his finger at her—he had to be telling
her not to touch it. Vera snatched her hand away.
Melody knew she wasn't imagining the look of
guilt on Vera's face.

"Come along, now, young ladies," Poppa said,
ushering them farther into the room. "Let's see
what kind of punch they make around here."

Melody accepted a little glass filled with bright
red liquid, then turned and caught her breath

sharply as she saw a man in a navy suit standing nearby, holding a cup of punch. It was the same man she'd bumped into earlier that day. The red-haired man.

"I myself had never seen one before." Mr. Whitelaw's voice carried above the murmur of the crowd. "It is a treasure. We are keeping it as carefully as the Elgin Marbles."

He certainly *was* hovering around it, Melody thought. He looked like he might eat it up if someone left him alone with it long enough.

"Yes, I'm flying out tomorrow morning on the early flight," Mr. Whitelaw said, continuing some other conversation. He trilled a laugh. "I was going to go next week, after the flower show ends, but the business there is urgent . . . well, of course Miami will be hot this time of year! But my business cannot wait."

His business . . . he was going to Miami tomorrow morning. Melody held her breath. *Oh my Lord, the orchid,* she thought feverishly. What if—could he be the thief? Was he going to steal the slipper orchid and take it to Miami to sell? *Look at how he's hovering over it!*

Melody grabbed Val's arm. "Val!" she whispered urgently.

"Ow!" Val rubbed her arm. "Easy there."

Before she could say anything more, Val stiffened, and Melody looked around to see Leah approaching. She was wearing a soft, pale blue chiffon dress that looked just like the one the actress Ann-Margret wore in the movie *Bye Bye Birdie.* Melody sighed in admiration.

"Hi," Melody greeted Leah. "Listen, I have to tell you guys something." But the words were hardly out of her mouth before she realized how sick Leah looked. Her face was pale and looked clammy. She folded and unfolded her lips in a way Melody had never seen before.

"Are you feeling all right?" Melody asked.

Leah jumped. "What? What did you say?"

Melody laid a hand on Leah's arm. "I just asked if you were sick. You don't look very well."

"Do you want a piece of peppermint gum?" Val offered, opening her purse. "My mom always says it helps settle your stomach."

Melody beamed at Val, who gave her a small—but real—smile in response.

Leah burped suddenly. "Excuse me. I need the bathroom." She rushed toward the ladies' room near the front of the rotunda.

"Whoa," Val said. "Good thing she didn't throw up right here."

Before Melody could reply, she heard a woman saying, "So nice to see you, Melody!" and turned to see Leah's mother supporting Dr. Roth, who was wearing a threadbare tuxedo. "You girls look lovely," Mrs. Roth smiled at them. "Is your mother here too, Val?"

"No, Poppa brought us," Val told her. "We're

his dates." She waved at Poppa, who made his way over to them.

"Melody, my dear, have you seen the lady's slipper orchid?" Dr. Roth asked, twinkling his eyes at Melody and leaning heavily on his cane. "Do you think it's the most beautiful flower in the room?"

"Yes," Melody told him. "It really is."

"We are so lucky you have lent it for tonight, Dad," Leah's mother said. "Now, I want you to sit down, right over here, and I'll bring you a glass of punch." She guided Dr. Roth over to a bench. He looked over his shoulder and gave Melody a little wave and a wink.

Val leaned over. "I have to go to the ladies' room. Do you know where it is?"

"Yeah, I'll go with you," Melody said. "We can see how Leah is, too." A sudden thought struck her. "We can check the orchid room for clues while we're there—it's right by the bathrooms. It was all blocked off this morning, but maybe they have it open now."

The noise of the party grew muted behind them as they ran down the little hallway and pushed through the door into the warm, humid air of the orchid room. Silence enfolded them. The room was deserted, and the only sound was the burble of water in the little stream.

Immediately, Melody noticed the bare spots on the shelves where the beautiful, rare orchids had stood only the day before. She darted a glance over her shoulder. The room was still deserted, but someone could come in at any moment. Quickly, she hoisted herself up on the low stone wall that wove through the room and peered at the shelves. There were round marks where the pots had stood, and some light, scattered soil. That was all.

"Do you see anything strange or suspicious?" Melody asked Val, who was searching the floor for clues.

"What's this?" Val picked up a little wad of paper from behind the door. It looked like it might have gotten pushed there when the door was opened. Val smoothed it out. "It's something . . . like a code with funny letters."

Melody hopped down from the wall and looked over Val's shoulder as she inspected the paper. Strange blocky shapes were scrawled on the dirty paper, as if someone had written them in a hurry. Suddenly, Melody knew where she'd seen letters like that before.

chapter 12

Hiding in Plain Sight

"IT'S HEBREW," MELODY blurted, squinting at the letters as if willing herself to understand them. "I saw writing like this at Leah's house. Maybe Dr. Roth will read it for us. Let's go ask him."

"Shouldn't we check on Leah first?" Val asked as she tucked the paper into her purse.

"Right, of course. Let's see how she's feeling."

As they neared the restrooms, Melody noticed two people standing in the lobby behind a big potted fern, arguing. She could hear their raised voices over the crowd, though not what they were saying. But as she and Val drew near, she could see that it was Leah and a man with a familiar baritone voice, his red hair bright above his navy suit. Leah appeared to be crying. As Melody watched, the red-haired man reached out and shook Leah's arm—hard.

Melody grabbed Val's shoulder. "Did you see that? What's that man doing to Leah?" Melody asked.

"Hey!" Val shouted and started forward. Leah and the man looked up, startled. Then the red-haired man turned and stepped away into the crowd, looking back at the girls with a calm smile.

They hurried over to Leah. "What was going on with that man, Leah?" Val asked her. "Why did he grab you like that?"

Melody felt Leah's hands the way Mommy did sometimes. "You're all clammy and sweaty! Are you okay? Do you want me to get your mother?"

"No!" Leah clutched at Melody with sudden vehemence. "No, don't say anything to my mother, please. She'll make me leave, and I can't! I just can't." Her voice trailed off, and she started to cry weakly, like a child, her hands pressed to her eyes.

Melody stood in shock. Her sophisticated,

mature friend! "Hey, it's okay," she managed to say soothingly. She patted Leah's shoulder while her eyes met Val's. *What on earth is going on?* She asked with her eyes.

I have no idea, Val silently answered back with a tiny shrug.

Leah gave a big sniff and blew her nose on the handkerchief Melody handed her. "I—I'm okay now," she said weakly. "Really. Sorry. I don't know what's wrong with me. Probably just stomach flu."

Not like any stomach flu I've ever seen, Melody thought.

Then Leah froze. Her eyes were wide as she stared over Melody's shoulder.

Melody turned around to look. Leah's mother was motioning the girls over with a big smile on her face—and the red-haired man right beside her.

"Girls!" Mrs. Roth called. "Come over—look who Zayde ran into."

Slowly, Leah walked over to her mother and

grandfather, who were still standing beside the slipper orchid. Melody and Val followed close behind.

"My dear, do you remember Harry Muntz? You met him a few months ago." Dr. Roth patted the sleeve of the red-haired man, whose face wore the same bland smile Melody remembered from outside the conservatory. Dr. Roth turned to Melody. "Harry is the son of my dear friend Norman Muntz, who was on the boat from Poland with me," he explained. "You recall I told you about Norman the day you visited Leah—he helped me escape from Poland and come to America. Harry found me recently, and we had a delightful visit at a coffee shop with Leah."

"Hello," Leah said. To Melody's surprise, her voice was smooth and impersonal, showing no sign of her illness—or that she recalled having met Mr. Muntz. She shook his outstretched hand. "Nice to see you again."

"Likewise, young lady," Mr. Muntz replied. His

voice was the same deep, pleasant baritone that Melody remembered from earlier encounters.

Melody, still feeling shocked and disoriented, tried not to stare at Leah. Why were they acting like they'd never met? They'd just been arguing! And they'd argued before, that day in the alley. Leah knew him!

Val suddenly trod on Melody's toe. "What's going on?" she whispered. "Why's she playing dumb?"

On the other side of the orchid, Mr. Whitelaw glanced in Melody's direction and did a double take. He looked flushed, and even from a short distance, Melody could see the sweat glistening on his face. He narrowed his eyes at her and drew himself up straight. Melody stared boldly back at him. He had a lot of nerve giving *her* dirty looks, thought Melody, when *he* was probably the one who had stolen the orchids!

After a few minutes of chit-chat, Mr. Muntz excused himself to get more punch. Poppa came over, and Melody introduced him to Leah's mother, while Dr. Roth rested on a folding chair nearby.

"I'm going to go sit down," Leah said weakly. She walked slowly toward the benches by the front doors.

Melody kept her eyes fixed on Mr. Whitelaw. He suddenly glanced at his watch, broke away from the knot of people he was conversing with, went over to a long row of light switches on a nearby wall, and dimmed the rotunda lights. Beside Melody, the lady's slipper orchid, spotlit on its special stand, seemed to glow even more brightly without the background light. Melody felt someone at her elbow and turned. It was Leah.

"Hey! Are you feeling better?" Melody asked, surprised.

"Yeah," Leah said, though her face was still pale. "I got worried about the orchid with so many people here."

Melody was burning inside with questions

about Harry Muntz. She suspected Leah wouldn't want to answer them, but Melody couldn't hold them back. "Leah, that Mr. Muntz—why were the two of you—"

Suddenly, Leah stumbled as if someone had bumped her, and she lurched against the velvet rope. The stanchions and rope crashed to the floor, taking the plant stand with it. The orchid hit the stone floor, the pot cracking and soil spilling out. "Oh! Oh!" Leah cried. People nearby gasped. Melody stood frozen in shock.

Mr. Whitelaw ran toward them, his mouth open in a round *O* and his hands outstretched. "What have you done?" he shouted as he lifted the orchid up from the floor, cradling it in his hands, elbowing Leah out of the way. Nearby, Melody saw Dr. Roth struggling to rise to his feet.

"Excuse me, excuse me!" Mr. Whitelaw was working his way through the crowd, the orchid in its cracked pot dribbling a trail of potting soil.

People parted to let him through, staring and whispering.

Melody, her heart pounding out of her chest, slipped through the crowd like a blade sliding through water. Could Mr. Whitelaw—an orchid collector himself—be stealing the lady's slipper? *He'll take the orchid out,* thought Melody, *and then tell everyone it was broken and dead. Then it will be his!*

Melody scanned the room for Leah but couldn't find her. Val stood near Poppa, her hands over her mouth. Melody wanted to go over to them but knew she mustn't let Mr. Whitelaw out of her sight. Ducking between people, she caught a glimpse of the botanist disappearing through a green unmarked door set discreetly into the wall. As she made her way toward it, another figure opened the green door: the red-headed man, Harry Muntz. And then, to her surprise, Melody saw Leah follow Mr. Muntz through the door.

Melody forced herself to wait a moment, to let

them get ahead. She didn't have time to grab Val—
she would have to go alone, and go now. She pulled
open the green door and let it wheeze shut behind
her. She stood an instant, trying to get her bear-
ings. She was in a long, dimly lit hallway leading to
the back rooms of the conservatory. There was no
sound except for the distant drip of water. Then—
footsteps, coming from the end of the passage.

Thinking fast, Melody pried off her hard-soled
dress shoes and tiptoed along the hallway on silent,
stockinged feet, staying close to the wall. A shadowy
figure crossed across the far end of the hall holding
an object—a man in a dark suit—Mr. Whitelaw with
the orchid. Melody hurried after him down the hall
and spotted him turning into a doorway.

Melody hurried down the hall and through the
doorway. Mr. Whitelaw stood at a counter in what
looked like some kind of potting room. Melody
watched, frozen, as he lifted the orchid out of the
cracked pot. Her teeth clenched with fear, Melody

stepped forward, then hesitated. Somehow, she had to stop him—

Suddenly, a loud bang came from the other end of the room, as if a door had flown open, and the room went dark.

Shadowy figures ran past. Stumbling, Melody backed away. Her palms hit the wall behind her, and she crouched against it. Someone grabbed someone else. She heard a cry. She couldn't see anything. The lights, where were the lights? Her hand groped the wall—there! She flicked the switch.

Leah and Harry Muntz stood in the middle of the room, scuffling. The orchid lay beside them on a long table. Pushing Leah away with one arm, Mr. Muntz reached for the orchid as Leah tried to grab it out of his hands.

"Put it down," Mr. Whitelaw called sharply.

Melody screamed. Harry Muntz spun around and ran, the orchid in one hand, its roots and petals dangling. His feet slipped on the polished floor and he hit a chair and fell. The orchid skidded across the floor. Leah dove to the floor, her hands scrabbling for the precious plant.

"Leah!" Melody cried, pressing her hands to her mouth. Her feet were rooted to the floor. Mr. Whitelaw snatched up the orchid, cradling it to his chest. Mr. Muntz rose heavily to his knees, bleeding slightly from a cut above his eye. Leah still lay on the floor, sobbing into her arms.

"Leah-leh? What are you doing here? Harry? What's happening?" Dr. Roth hobbled through the door with Leah's mother right behind him. Dr. Roth bent over Leah, trying to pull her up, trembling with the effort.

Leah raised her head. Her eyes, streaming tears, found Melody's, and Melody read the truth there. It was Leah who had stolen the orchids—Leah and Mr. Muntz.

"You?" Melody gasped. "But—why?"

Leah nodded. "I can explain . . ." she whispered.

The strength drained suddenly from Melody's legs, and she sat down in a nearby chair with a thump.

All this time she'd been trying to find the thief. And the thief had been hiding right in front of her, in plain sight.

chapter 13

Confession

MELODY PERCHED ON the edge of a metal folding chair. Mommy held Melody's hand on one side of her, and on the other, Daddy gave her a reassuring smile. Poppa and Val sat on folding chairs, too, with Poppa's arm laid protectively across Val's shoulders. All of them were squeezed into a cramped little cinder block room in the police station. Harsh fluorescent light glared down on them. Dr. Roth sat at the end of the row with his head bowed, both hands resting on his cane.

Leah, her mother, and Harry Muntz weren't there. When they'd arrived, they had been whisked into another room.

After the scene in the back room at the conservatory, Mr. Whitelaw had called the police. He had led the group quietly out the side door of the conservatory, and three squad cars had ferried the group downtown. Mommy and Daddy had met Melody at the station, where they'd all been escorted into the cinder block room and told to wait. That was half an hour ago.

Suddenly, the heavy door opened. Leah and her mother entered, followed by Officer Baer. Leah's eyes were swollen from crying. The metal chairs screeched on the floor as Mrs. Roth sat down beside her daughter. Their faces were pale and drawn.

Officer Baer cleared his throat. "This young lady has been very cooperative. She has told us in detail of her actions over the past twenty-four hours, and now she has asked that she be permitted to explain her actions to all of you." He pulled out a chair as well and sat down, crossing his arms over his chest.

No one said anything. A clock above the door ticked steadily. Then Dr. Roth leaned over and took one of Leah's hands. "My dear," he said. That was all, but his voice held such love that Melody's eyes welled up. Leah must have felt the same way, because tears started streaming down her cheeks. She looked up at her grandfather.

"It was all for you!" she whispered.

"Was it, my dear?" Dr. Roth's brows knitted.

Mrs. Roth said gently, "Why don't you start at the beginning, honey?"

Leah took a deep breath. "Zayde, do you remember the day Harry Muntz called you back in February?" she asked her grandfather.

"Yes, I remember that. He called out of the blue and said that he was Norman Muntz's son and would like to meet and talk about his father." Dr. Roth turned to Officer Baer, explaining, "Norman was a dear friend of mine—we escaped Poland together—so of course I wanted to meet his son Harry. We met at a coffee shop on our street. Leah came along to help me walk there and back."

Leah looked miserable as she continued her

account. "The thing is, Zayde, Harry Muntz didn't really want to talk to you about his father. What he really wanted was the lady's slipper orchid, and that's the reason he looked you up. He told me that he's a dealer in orchids and rare plants. He remembered his father's stories about your orchid, and he knew how valuable it would be if it was still alive."

"But—but—" Dr. Roth looked utterly baffled. Melody felt the same way. "My dear, how could you possibly know these things?" Dr. Roth stammered.

Leah spread her hands in front of her on the table. "Harry Muntz is a very smart man, Zayde. He saw how sick you were, and he must have seen how worried I was about you. I—I have a hard time hiding it."

That's true, Melody thought. She remembered how obvious it was to her from the start that Leah was crazy about her grandpa—and worried about him, too.

Leah went on. "After the visit in the coffee shop,

Mr. Muntz waited for me outside the apartment one day. He said he had to talk with me, and he showed me this." Leah pulled a crumpled magazine clipping from her purse. She gave it to Dr. Roth, who read it quietly, then handed it to Poppa, then Melody.

Melody scanned the article. "Dr. Edwards Receives $1.2 Million Grant," the headline announced. "Dr. Timothy Edwards of the Memorial Sloan Kettering Hospital in New York City has been awarded a $1.2 million grant from the National Institutes of Health to study the effects of long-term starvation in survivors of World War II and the Holocaust. Dr. Edwards has pioneered groundbreaking treatment of these survivors . . ." Melody looked up as Leah continued speaking.

"Mr. Muntz told me that if I helped him steal your orchid, we could sell it for enough money to fly you to New York. He could tell that we didn't have the money for something like that. But I couldn't let him have your orchid! I told him that it was dead. That's when he suggested that we—" Leah's voice dropped— "steal orchids from the conservatory," she mumbled. Flushing, she looked down at her lap.

Silence draped the room.

"Mr. Muntz is really the criminal here," Leah's mother said quietly. She put her hand on Leah's and looked at her daughter. "You have made some bad choices, but Mr. Muntz took advantage of your love for Zayde for his own financial gain, and that's despicable."

Leah looked up at her mother with watery eyes. "I'm so, so sorry. I knew what I was doing was wrong—I felt sick because it was so wrong. But I had to get the money somehow, and I couldn't think of any other way to get it. Babysitting for the Myers wasn't bringing in enough."

"So, what—you commit a crime for this?" Dr. Roth asked in disbelief.

"Why didn't you talk to Zayde and me?" Mrs. Roth added. "Why did you keep your worries a secret?"

"I did talk to Zayde, and he said it wasn't worth the money," Leah told them. "So I thought if I could just *get* the money—I figured a trip to New York would cost about nine hundred dollars, and then the cost of the treatment would be more . . ." Her voice cracked.

Melody thought she might cry, too, along with her friend. To think that Leah was so scared of her grandfather dying that she'd steal to try to help him! At the same time, anger poked at her. If Leah hadn't been caught, would she have just let Poppa take the blame for the crime?

Leah wiped her nose on her sleeve. Val quickly opened her white purse and handed Leah a hanky. Leah took it, giving Val a tiny nod, and went on. "So we made a plan. Mr. Muntz would sell the orchids if I could get them out of the conservatory, and we would split the money. I met him the day of the Fair Housing Committee picnic. He came to look at the orchid room and the conservatory layout."

"I saw him that day," Melody said suddenly. Everyone looked at her. "I saw a man examining the lock on the side door. He had red hair. It was him."

Leah nodded and then turned to her grandfather. "Friday evening at the conservatory, when you were meeting with Mr. Whitelaw to prepare for your lecture, I went into the orchid room, took the orchids Harry Muntz had pointed out to me, slipped them into shopping bags, and handed them out the side door. In all the commotion with the show setup, no one noticed me, or him outside in the dark. He just took the shopping bags to his car and drove away."

Melody thought back to Friday night—was it really only yesterday?—and remembered that at one point Leah had suddenly disappeared. Melody had gone to look for her in the gift shop, and then the bathroom—which was right by the orchid room. Leah had appeared a few moments later in the hallway, all hot and sweaty. What was it she had said to Melody? *Just getting some fresh air . . . it's so hot in here.*

Val spoke up. "We found this in the orchid room today," she said, holding out the dirty piece of paper with Hebrew letters.

Leah glanced at the paper as Officer Baer took it from Val. "I didn't know I'd dropped it," she said. "Harry Muntz made notes for me on which orchids to take—he made them in Hebrew, like a code." She took a long, shaky breath. "But then, today, Mr. Muntz told me the conservatory orchids weren't enough. He said he couldn't sell those five orchids for more than three hundred dollars each, even though I knew they were worth more. And of course he was keeping half. I needed more than seven hundred and fifty dollars, but I didn't want to steal again. I begged him to loan me some money and promised to pay him back from my babysitting wages, but he refused. We argued about it at the Soiree." She looked at Melody. "I think you saw us."

Melody nodded. "I saw you arguing in the alley the day we handed out the fliers, too."

"Yes. He wanted more of the take. We'd agreed on two-thirds for me and one-third for him, but then he changed his mind. He said he'd be taking half . . . and there was nothing I could do about it. I needed the money, so I had to accept his terms." Leah paused as if to gather strength to continue her story, and then went on.

"I was trying to do everything I could to keep him from seeing the lady's slipper. I knew he'd want it as soon as he saw it. I tried to keep you from bringing it to the lecture, Zayde." Her voice fell to a cracked whisper. "I tried. And when he spotted it tonight at the Soiree, I could tell he was planning to take it, somehow."

Melody's mind hummed, putting it all together. That's why Leah had been so upset when Dr. Roth offered to bring the lady's slipper to the lecture. That's why she'd looked as though she was going to pass out at the party when they were all talking to Harry Muntz. And that's why she'd acted as if she didn't know him.

After a moment, Leah went on. "I knew I had to try to get to the lady's slipper before he did. I bumped the plant stand on purpose at the party—I knew Mr. Whitelaw would take the orchid out. But then Muntz followed him. I went after them. Muntz knew there was another door into the potting room. He went in that way and turned the lights out. I figured he was going to grab the orchid and run with it in the confusion. I tried to stop him—and Melody turned on the lights."

Leah looked over at Melody. Melody thought

she'd never felt so confused. She had wanted to catch the thief, but she hadn't wanted to catch *Leah*. And yet, because she had, now Poppa was safe. His shop was safe. The lady's slipper orchid was safe. But what would happen to Leah?

"Leah . . . I'm sorry," Melody whispered. She hoped Leah would know what she meant.

Leah came up with a watery little smile. "That's what I get for choosing smart friends." Then she added, "Melody, I wanted to tell you everything after you met Zayde. I knew I could trust you to keep a big secret. But I was afraid you wouldn't want to be friends with me if you knew what I was planning to do."

Melody didn't know what to say, so she was silent. But Leah wasn't finished.

"And then—" Leah's voice wavered, but she cleared her throat and continued, "when you told me your grandfather was being questioned—and I knew it was only because—because—oh, Melody, it was terrible!" She began to weep. "It's like what the Nazis did to Zayde, arresting him not because he'd done anything but simply because he was Jewish!" Leah broke into huge, racking sobs. The sound of her weeping echoed off the walls. She dropped her head into her arms on her lap and cried and cried. Melody had never heard anyone sound so sad.

"Oh, my dear girl. The world can be a hard place." Dr. Roth put his hand on his granddaughter's head. When her sobs had quieted some, he said, "My dear, the damage to my health was done long ago, and it is here to stay. It's not just a matter of money or medicine. I've been to many doctors, and I'm afraid no treatment, no specialist can fix me. But my darling Leah, you have forgotten something very important."

"What?" Leah's voice was muffled in her arms.

"I have had a long life, and a good life—wonderful, in fact. Yes, we suffered in Europe, but I have had a wonderful life here in America. I lost my son too young, but I have had you and your mother, and I have had the great good luck to live to be an old man. So many of my friends and family in Poland never had that chance—never saw their children grow up and get married, never knew their grand-children. I am a lucky man. And a happy man. And when it is my time to go, well, then, I will go in peace." Dr. Roth raised Leah's tear-streaked face with one hand. "You must accept that, Leah-leh. No matter how much you want to keep me here."

The tears were streaming down Melody's face as well. Mommy handed her a tissue, and then blot-ted her own eyes.

After a silence, Leah's mother spoke up. "Where is Harry Muntz?"

"He's still being questioned," Officer Baer replied. "So far, his story supports Miss Roth's here." The officer cleared his throat and turned to Poppa. "Mr. Porter, needless to say, you won't be charged."

"I'm glad for that." Poppa looked exhausted, but relieved.

Officer Baer rose and held the door as the group filed out. Melody looked back at Leah, sitting with her mother and grandfather, her head bowed.

"Leah," she said quietly. Her friend looked up. "Call me later?"

Leah gave Melody a little smile. She nodded. "Yeah. Yes. I will."

Out on the sidewalk, the night air was cool and damp. Poppa, Mommy, Daddy, Val, and Melody climbed into Daddy's car.

"Daddy, what will happen to Leah?" Melody asked as they drove down the nighttime street. On either side, the houses sat quiet and full of sleep.

"She'll have to appear in court," Daddy said. "She will likely be charged with a crime. She's a minor, so she'll probably just be sentenced to perform some community service."

"It's a shame, a fine young girl like that," said Mommy. "She must have felt truly desperate."

"I think she did," Val spoke up. Melody stared at her cousin. Was Val defending Leah?

"I mean, I might do the same thing for Poppa, if he was sick and we needed lots of money to cure him," Val went on.

"I hope not, baby," Poppa said from the front seat.

"I'm glad you understand Leah," Melody said to Val. "You know, she told me about what happened to her grandpa in Poland—he was put in a ghetto by the Nazis and almost starved to death. And it ruined his health forever. She asked me not to tell anyone; that's the secret I was keeping. It wasn't a secret *from you,* it was a secret *for her*—do you see what I mean?"

Val nodded slowly. "Yeah, I do. Friends are supposed to keep each other's secrets. I'd always want you to keep mine."

"And I would!" Melody said fervently. "I just wanted to be a good friend to Leah—that was all. I swear."

"I know that now, Dee-Dee." Val squeezed her hand, and Melody felt the last bits of tension between them melt away. She sighed with relief and leaned back against the cushion of the backseat.

"Maybe we can go over to see Leah in a day or two," Val mused. The night skyline sparkled through the window behind her. "I think she could probably use some friends."

"Yeah, let's do that," Melody agreed. She paused, reflecting on all the events of the past week. "Boy, that slipper orchid sure is something. I can see why people might pay a lot of money for it."

"It's like a rare jewel," Val agreed.

"Still, all the orchids are beautiful, even the ones that aren't so valuable. Don't you think so, Poppa?" Melody asked.

"Yes," Poppa replied. "In fact, I'm thinking of

stocking a few orchids in my flower shop."

"Oh, no, Poppa, are you sure you want to, after what happened?" Melody said anxiously.

"Now, now," Poppa said. "We won't have any of them high-falutin' lady's slippers. Just common orchids—the kind that won't cause *any* trouble."

Despite the long, difficult day, Melody's heart lifted. That was her Poppa, finding a hint of humor even in a dark moment. Melody suddenly felt flooded with relief and gratitude for her family. She caught Val's eye, and they shared their special cousin smile.

INSIDE Melody's World

During her adventures on Belle Isle, Melody discovers how fascinating orchids can be. There are more than 25,000 orchid species; many are very beautiful, and some are quite strange and unusual in the plant world. For example, the blossom of the *Satyrium pumilum* smells like rotting meat to attract flies that will pollinate the plant. The *Ophrys bombyliflora* produces a blossom that looks like a female bumblebee to attract bees as pollinators. And the *Dracula simia* orchid appears to have a tiny monkey's face in the middle of the blossom.

Because of their beauty and elegance, orchids are popular, and rare ones can be quite valuable. Today, a single stem of Rothschild's slipper orchid sells for as much as $5,000. Because of the flowers' value, orchid poachers in Melody's time and today search the world for rare species, take them from their native habitat without permission, and sell them on the black market before botanists have had a chance to preserve and study them.

Melody discovered the shady world of orchid theft while she was visiting Belle Isle, a 900-acre island in the middle of the Detroit River. Belle Isle, which means "beautiful island" in French, has always been a special place to Detroiters. In Melody's day, families would drive to the island for a green, cool respite from the heat and noise of summertime Detroit. Some families would sleep out on Belle Isle under the stars on hot summer nights.

In addition to the beach, zoo, aquarium, and other attractions, there was the conservatory, with its 85-foot-tall glass-and-steel dome. In 1953, the newspaper heiress Anna Scripps Whitcomb gave the conservatory her collection of 600 orchids. As Poppa explains in the story, the heiress had saved many of these orchids from destruction by bringing them from England to the United States during World War II.

Unlike the orchids, many treasures did not make it out of wartime Britain and Europe. The Nazis drove millions of Jewish families from their homes and businesses and then looted their possessions, stealing art, jewelry, and heirlooms. Desperate Jews hid their valuables wherever they could, just as Dr. Roth concealed his orchid cutting. As recently as 2016, the staff at a museum in Poland discovered a gold necklace and ring hidden under a false bottom in a mug that had been used by a prisoner at Auschwitz, a Nazi concentration camp.

Melody learns important lessons during the Belle Isle Flower Show. She learns that ugliness and beauty can be twined together like two vines: Leah's deception and her deep love for her grandfather; Dr. Roth's starvation by the Nazis and his escape to a good life in America; the greed of orchid smugglers and the beauty of orchids. Melody also learns more about the terrible results of racial stereotyping, which led to the Nazis' persecution of Jews as well as to the presumption that Poppa was guilty of stealing. And she sees that racial stereotyping hurts not only its immediate victims but also those who love them.

Read more of MELODY'S stories,

available from booksellers and at *americangirl.com*

♪ *Classics* ♪

Melody's classic series, now in two volumes:

Volume 1:

No Ordinary Sound

Melody can't wait to sing her first solo at church. She spends the summer practicing the perfect song—and helping her brother become a Motown singer. When an unimaginable tragedy leaves her silent, Melody has to find her voice.

Volume 2:

Never Stop Singing

Now that her brother is singing for Motown, Melody gets to visit a real recording studio. She also starts a children's block club. Melody is determined to help her neighborhood bloom—and make her community stronger.

♪ *Journey in Time* ♪

Travel back in time—and spend a few days with Melody!

Music in My Heart

Step into Melody's world of the 1960s! Volunteer with a civil rights group, join a demonstration, or use your voice to sing backup for a Motown musician! Choose your own path through this multiple-ending story.

♬ A Sneak Peek at ♬

No Ordinary
Sound

A Melody Classic

Volume 1

Melody's adventures begin in the
first volume of her classic stories.

Big Momma brought the roast in and everyone took their places around the table, with Poppa at one end and Daddy at the other. With Yvonne home from college, the family was truly all together, the way their Sundays used to be.

"Did you study all the time, Vonnie?" Melody asked. Mommy had gone to college at Tuskegee, and this year Dwayne had applied and been accepted. Melody knew that her parents hoped all their children would graduate from Tuskegee one day, too.

Yvonne shook her head so that her small earrings sparkled. "There's so much more to do at school besides studying," she said, reaching for more gravy.

"Like what?" Poppa asked, propping his elbows on the table. Melody held back a giggle when she saw Big Momma frown the same way Mommy had, but Poppa paid no attention.

"Well, last week before finals a bunch of us went out to help black people in the community register to vote," Yvonne said. "And do you know, a lady told me she was too afraid to sign up."

"Why was she afraid?" Melody interrupted.

"Because somebody threw a rock through her next-door neighbor's window after her neighbor voted," Yvonne explained, her eyes flashing with anger. "This is 1963! How can anybody get away with that?"

Melody looked from Yvonne to her father. "You always say not voting is like not being able to talk. Why wouldn't anybody want to talk?"

Daddy sighed. "It's not that she doesn't want to vote, Melody. There are a lot of unfair rules down South that keep our people from exercising their rights. Some white people will do anything, including scaring black people, to keep change from happening. They don't want to share jobs or neighborhoods or schools with us. Voting is like a man or woman's voice speaking out to change those laws and rules."

"And it's not just about voting," Mommy said. "Remember what Rosa Parks did in Montgomery? She stood up for her rights."

"You mean she *sat down* for her rights," Melody said. Melody knew all about Mrs. Parks, who got arrested for simply sitting down on a city bus. She had paid her fare like everybody else, but because she was a Negro the bus driver told her she had to give her seat to a white person! *But that happened eight years ago,* Melody realized. *Why haven't things changed?*

"Aren't we just as good as anybody else?" Melody asked as she looked around the table. "The laws should be fair everywhere, for everybody, right?"

"That's not always the way life works," Poppa said.

"Why not?" Lila asked.

Poppa sat back and rubbed his silvery mustache. That always meant he was about to tell a story.

"Back in Alabama, there was a white farmer who owned the land next to ours. Palmer was his name. Decent fellow. We went into town the same day to sell our peanut crops. It wasn't a good growing year, but I'd lucked out with twice as many sacks of peanuts as Palmer. Well, at the market they counted and weighed his sacks. Then they counted and weighed my sacks. Somehow Palmer got twice as much money as I got for selling half the crop I had. They never even checked the quality of what we had, either."

"What?" Lila blurted out.

"How?" Melody scooted to the edge of her chair.

"Wait, now." Poppa waved his grandchildren quiet. "I asked the man to weigh it again, but he refused. I complained. Even Palmer spoke up for me. But that man turned to me and said, 'Boy—'"

"He called you *boy*?" Dwayne interrupted, putting his fork down.

"'Boy,'" Poppa continued, "'this is all you're gonna get. And if you keep up this trouble, you won't have any farm to go back to!'"

Melody's mouth fell open. "What was he talking about? You did have a farm," she said, glancing at Big Momma.

"He meant we were in danger of losing our farm—our home—because your grandfather spoke out to a white man," Big Momma explained. She shook her head slowly. "As hard as we'd worked to buy that land, as hard as it was for colored people to own anything in Alabama, we decided that day that we had to sell and move north."

Although Melody had heard many of her grandfather's stories about life in Alabama before, she'd never heard this one. And as she considered it, she realized that on their many trips down South, she'd never seen the old family farm. Maybe her grandparents didn't want to go back.

Melody sighed. Maybe the lady Yvonne mentioned didn't want to risk losing *her* home if she "spoke out" by voting. But Yvonne was right—it was hard to understand how that could happen in the United States of America in 1963!

Poppa was shaking his head. "It's a shame that colored people today still have to be afraid of standing up or speaking out for themselves."

"Negroes," Mommy corrected him.

"Black people," Yvonne said firmly.

"Well, what *are* we supposed to call ourselves?" Lila asked.

Melody thought about how her grandparents usually said "colored." They were older and from the South, and Big Momma said that's what was proper when they were growing up. Mommy and Daddy mostly said "Negroes." But ever since she went to college, Yvonne was saying "black people." Melody noticed that Mommy and Daddy were saying it sometimes, too. She liked the way it went with "white people," like a matched set. But sometimes she wished they didn't need all these color words at all. Melody spoke up. "What about 'Americans'?" she said.

Yvonne still seemed upset. "That's right, Dee-Dee. We're Americans. We have the same rights as white Americans. There shouldn't be any separate water fountains or waiting rooms or public bathrooms. Black Americans deserve equal treatment and equal pay. And sometimes we have to remind people."

"How do we remind them?" Lila asked. Melody was wondering the same thing.

"By not shopping at stores that won't hire black workers," Yvonne explained. "By picketing in front of a restaurant that won't serve black people. By marching."

"You won't catch me protesting or picketing or marching in any street," Dwayne interrupted, working on his third helping of potatoes. "I'm gonna be onstage or in the recording studio, making music and getting famous."

Mr. Ellison shook his head, and Melody knew there was going to be another argument, the way there always was when Dwayne talked about becoming a music star.

About the Author

At first, EMMA CARLSON BERNE
thought she was going to be a college
professor, so she went to graduate school
at Miami University in Ohio. After that,
she taught horseback riding in Boston and
Charleston, South Carolina. *Then* Emma
found out how much she enjoys writing for
children and young adults. Since that time,
she has authored more than two dozen books
and often writes about historical figures such
as Sacagawea, Helen Keller, Christopher
Columbus, and the artist Frida Kahlo.
Emma lives in a hundred-year-old house
in Cincinnati, Ohio, with her three children
and her husband.